*The Legend of SeaWalker* is dedicated to my mom Darlene, my brothers Steve, Bill and Tom, and my whole family. Steve Creech, President of the Wyland Foundation, a great writer who helped me flush out some cool stuff here. Also my great Art Director Gregg Hamby and friends who helped edit my first book of fiction. To my millions of collectors and fans throughout the U.S. and around the world . I hope you enjoy the first of my three part series. Thanks to all!

-Wyland

# THE LEGEND OF SEAWALKER

WRITTEN BY

# WYLAND

NEW YORK

LONDON • NASHVILLE • MELBOURNE • VANCOUVER

# THE LEGEND OF SEAWALKER

Published in New York, New York, by Morgan James Publishing. Morgan James is a trademark of Morgan James, LLC. www.MorganJamesPublishing.com

ISBN 9781642799576 paperback
ISBN 9781642799583 case laminate
ISBN 9781642799590 eBook
Library of Congress Control Number: 2019919937

Morgan James is a proud partner of Habitat for Humanity Peninsula and Greater Williamsburg. Partners in building since 2006.

Get involved today! Visit
MorganJamesPublishing.com/giving-back

# CONTENTS

v

# CONTENTS

# CONTENTS

TO BE CONTINUED...

# INTRODUCTION
## BY SeaWalker

I really don't remember much, only that I was moving around in a large bubble in salty water. This was my first memory as I seemed to metamorphosize like a caterpillar into a butterfly. If it sounds strange, it really was. Imagine how I felt being transformed from a baby into a new species... not human or dolphin but perhaps, somewhere in the middle, A hybrid really. My awareness immediately transformed. The first thing I saw through the bubble was not my parents but the smiling dolphins who were excited as they watched the transformation in a matter of minutes. I grew a dorsal fin along with webbed fingers and fins where feet had been. Dolphins are naturally curious, and this must've been something completely alien to them. It sure was for me! It felt like my molecules were exploding as I felt my human form changing to adapt to the ocean environment. Then suddenly the bubble burst, and I was floating weightless in the buoyant sea.

A group of young, strong dolphins were chattering excitedly among themselves. I too was curious. Where the heck was I, and who were these strange looking creatures who had taken to me like a new toy? I was certain these new, amazing and strong animals were there for a reason, one I would appreciate in the near future. Of all the creatures who could have found me in the unforgiving ocean home, I was rescued by perhaps the only creature that could have saved me. The dolphins would later tell me that they found me inside a bubble resting on the ocean floor. They knew instinctively to take me deeper into the ocean realm where all life began. Strange gases from the ancient sea floor transformed me into an aquatic creature that could survive the harsh elements that no human could normally survive! If a shark had saved me, I surely would've been eaten. But, with my good luck, it happened to be one of the most intelligent and strong animals that have thrived in the oceans for millions of years. I would always be grateful to my dolphin tribe, and we consider each other family as we face today's challenges of survival. Most threats were coming from one species, the humans in the above world. They were bringing the oceans to the brink as they continued to pollute and over fish with no regard for future generations or other species. I felt strongly that I had a role to play, learning everything I could in order to inspire positive action on behalf of the ocean's health.

I was reborn again in the buoyant sea. The future is uncertain. Could the humans and marine creatures coexist... now and in the future? One thing was for sure, I had good mentors. I considered the great whales and dolphins my family now, and they were sharing their wisdom with me each and every day so that one day I may change the world.

Each year, I learned more from all of the sea creatures. They continued to inspire me to make a difference, not only for my new family, but all life on the planet... the water planet. I certainly had the curious gene that dolphins possess – maybe even more so! I wanted to see the entire ocean realm and experience it firsthand. Some of the things I saw were unbelievable, and luckily, I survived. Some of the things were just weird and even scary. I want to share the stories with you and all the land walkers so everyone can see the big picture. The truth of the matter is that from the very beginning, all life began in the sea, and every species is controlled by biological factors. Only today, the balance of the sea is being pushed to its limits by one species... man! The great whales have always been the oracle of knowledge, an alien species that has been around since the time of the dinosaurs and before. The blue whale, the largest of all the great giants, was hunted to near extinction in the last century. These giants have always communicated over hundreds of miles through their echolocation. With their numbers diminished and the oceans becoming noisy because of giant ships, the whales are having trouble finding each other to mate and to share their knowledge. Another insult over the past few decades is whales and other marine life including dolphins being captured and put on display in captivity for human entertainment. My biggest fear is seeing my family disappear from their tribes never to be seen again.

I also saw some very bizarre alien behavior in the Bermuda triangle. Only today are we learning some of the strange occurrences that have happened here where the aliens are actually using the humans to support their own colonies in factories deep under the sea. I'm looking forward to telling you the story as we witness some unexplained phenomenon that is happening below the surface. Take my web hand, and follow me as I report some of the strange encounters that may one day affect all life on the planet.

*Spirits of the deep awaken to a new resident*
*born of the land and now of the sea...*

*W*

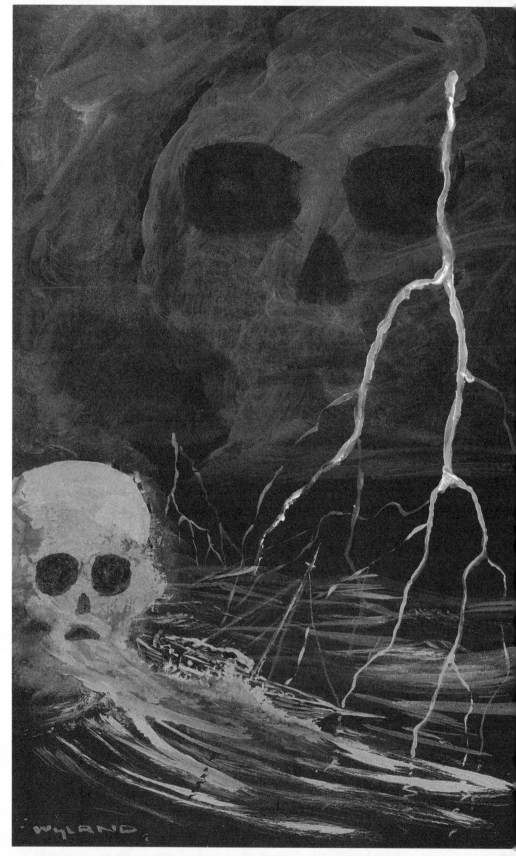

# CHAPTER ONE
# STORM

It was another perfect morning in the little town of Islamorada in the Florida Keys. Islamorada is a small drinking town with a big fishing problem, the locals liked to say. A young, married couple was planning to sail to the Caribbean for a short vacation like they had done many times before. Steve, husband and Captain, was a writer specializing in murder mysteries with three books published in the last few years, although he still made a living as a reporter for the Miami Herald. His bride of eighteen months, Ocean, had given them their first child, a beautiful little boy they would call Walker, Steve's middle name. They were water people; Steve liked to sail, and Ocean was a competitive college swimmer. Both were divers. They were even both water signs, he a Cancer and her a Pisces. In the eyes of many, they were the perfect couple, and now they had Walker.

This morning they would set sail for the Bahamas to introduce their new baby to the wild Atlantic bottlenose dolphins. Steve knew that dolphins were very curious of babies, and the couple was excited to share their love of the sea and dolphins with their new baby. It couldn't have been a more perfect day to sail. The conditions were ideal: flat sea, bright blue sky and pillow-like clouds swept by gentle breezes. The warm teal blue waters reflected the clouds above and revealed the coral reef below. The water was so clear that they could look over the side and see schools of reef fish and a green sea turtle that swam near the bow. They were also treated to several black frigate birds slowly drifting above, effortlessly flying in the airstream. Nothing was better than sailing these calm, warm tropical waters.

Steve and Ocean felt truly blessed as their forty-foot schooner, a boat they had named Celebration, left Florida Bay for an easy eight-hour voyage to the Bahamas. They met in college at the University of Miami during their freshman year. A mutual friend had set them up on a blind date and from that moment, it seemed they were never apart. Best of all, they shared the same deep connection to the sea. Sailing had been in Steve's family since his first ancestors came to America from their native home of Wales. So, it was only natural that the first major purchase they made as a couple was the vessel they had spent so many hours restoring. The couple enjoyed sitting together at the wheel gazing at the night sky as the Celebration glided through the calm waters of the Caribbean. They dreamed of the day when they could retire off of Steve's success as a published author. They had each other, their family and the future ahead of them. Life was about as good as it could be.

After a leisurely seven-hour sail, they entered the Bermuda

Triangle off the Bahamas. The stories of mystery appealed to the writer in Steve, which included tales of lost ships, flight squadrons and huge freighters disappearing without a trace. Of course, there were simple explanations for everything, Steve thought. But he had to admit that strange stories abounded here. He had learned never to take the sea for granted. As he thought about this, a gust of wind slammed against the sail. The boat jolted hard. He called down to Ocean, "You guys okay?"

"Yeah. What happened?" she answered.

"Wind's picking up."

He checked the horizon. The sky had darkened, as if someone had flipped a light switch. The once calm waters rippled and then churned with whitecaps across the horizon. Steve fought his impulse to turn around. Just go forward he thought. This will clear. But as the boat moved into the rough waters, a sense of dread flooded over him. The further the Celebration headed into the churning water, the more the sea raged and boiled. The boat turned, and they were thrust into an ear-piercing whirlpool of raging water covered by ominous skies. The beautiful, white animal shaped clouds that had kept them company all day had now turned low, dark and menacing. When Steve saw the approaching squall line, his heart sunk. The winds from squalls

# CHAPTER ONE

were very strong and savage, and they were as destructive as tornadoes. There was thunder, lighting and stinging sheets of rain. There was no time to warn Ocean before the storm hit. They could only hold on and pray. He yelled to Ocean, "Hang on!

Steve looked through the window. Ocean closed the hatch and swept the baby up into her arms. "The Devil's Triangle", as the area had often been called, was living up to its legendary reputation. Whatever this was, it was real. Now the question: would they make it through? The swells grew by the minute. Ten feet. Twenty feet. In minutes, it seemed the sea pitched in all directions. The swells were at fifty feet now and growing. Each moment it seemed the sea became angrier and darker. They were in a giant whirlpool, swirling like a washing machine in a category five hurricane.

Adrenalin fired through Steve's body. There was no time to think, no time to bring the sails down, no time to secure the ship. He couldn't even get a position. The needle of the ship's compass was spinning madly. The Celebration rose and bucked against the waves. Nothing Steve had learned prepared him for this. Everything– the sky, the sea, the wind – screamed with incomprehensible fury. He managed to feel his way to the radio to alert the Coast Guard or anyone listening on the ship's radio, turning quickly to the emergency frequency. The radio squeaked and wailed. "Mayday! Mayday!" Steve yelled. "This is Captain Steve Walker Jones of the schooner Celebration! We have an emergency situation! Please send immediate, emergency assistance! We are taking on massive amounts of water, and our engine is failing! My wife has a baby! Can you read me? Please respond!" As the radio squeaked louder, a strange voice came on with perfect clarity, "Please maintain your position," the voice said. "We are watching you."

Steve didn't understand. How was he to maintain position? There was no way to control the boat. No way to do anything. Ocean asked, "are we going to be okay?" She was frightened and scared as she opened the cabin door. Steve looked at her trying to hide his concern.

"We are going to be okay," he said. "We're going to be okay. I think they're sending a rescue vessel. Just take care of the baby." But he knew they were too far out. They needed help now. It was everything he could do now to save the vessel from going down. The sea was pitch black, and the billowing clouds of dark gray and fiery red told him that everything was decidedly not okay. A large shadow passed over the boat as a giant, tornado-like water spout sucked up the ocean and moved toward the Celebration. Another spout formed off the starboard side. The winds tore at what was left of the sails as the mast gave way and fell into the raging sea. It was as if the entire ocean was pulling at the vessel, trying to roll it over and drag it into the abyss. The seas had grown into rolling mountains that crashed relentlessly against the hull. The unthinkable was happening. Steve had to tell Ocean. "we're going down!" he shouted.

At that moment, the Celebration rolled over, and the sea began to devour it. In less than a minute, the vessel began to sink into the deep. Steve and Ocean were immediately separated by the unforgiving water. It was then that Steve was lost in the raging sea, pulled into the depth with unsustainable pressure.

The child was ripped from his mother's arms and enveloped in a blue light bubble that seemed to shield him from the ravages of the storm. He couldn't understand what was happening as his mother disappeared into the darkness, flung from the broken vessel. A quiet fell over the baby as he descended into the water, alongside the Celebration, which fell like a rock deeper and deeper into the bottom of the mysterious sea. The boy was now floating in a cocoon-like air blanket as the Celebration raced beside him toward the depth of the sea and finally crashed. The baby gasped the very last vestige of air in a black unforgiving sea.

*The Bermuda triangle now suddenly turned into the Devils triangle taking another ship and three more souls...*

*W*

# CHAPTER TWO

# GENESIS, BOY IN THE BUBBLE

The Celebration came to rest on the edge of a deep water canyon. The cocoon-like bubble that had carried the child gently landed on the soft bottom a hundred yards away. The bubbles' air was now replaced with the very gases that formed the first life on the water planet. It seemed to calm him, even as the elements inside the bubble began to rapidly change. There was no way to tell how much time had passed. The air felt different now. It was heavier and denser, but comfortable, as though he was born to it. His senses opened to faint sounds around him. Far away, he sensed movement and life. Slowly, the boy was becoming something much different. He was metamorphosing into a completely different being.

Despite the pleasant way the bubble made him feel, he still felt he had lost something terribly important. He reached outward for the hands that had always responded lovingly, but this time, there was nothing to hold him. Something inside told him to let the feeling go. There was no need to remember it anymore. But the sadness overwhelmed him, and perhaps for the final time, he began to cry. And, as he did, he saw large shadows encircle his bubble. The shadows grew larger until they filled

# CHAPTER TWO

the child's vision. He felt curious. When he touched the side of the cocoon, one of the shadows pushed gently in response. This call and response continued. Every time the boy touched the side, the shadows would push, as if it were a game. With a flash, the cocoon pulsed a warning. Whatever was out there was not welcome. But the boy felt differently. He sensed the mind of the cocoon claiming him and the presence of the shadows outside beckoning him in a completely different way.

The shadowy creatures now worked quickly as a group before the cocoon could flash again. They tore at the cocoon to free the boy. The smile of an Atlantic bottlenose dolphin appeared, then another, then another. In seconds, the boy's entire world was filled with dolphins. They lifted him and nudged him, and the boy responded instinctively by kicking his legs. Each time he kicked, he zoomed through the water at an incredible speed. As his vision adapted, he glanced at his legs and his arms and noted the silvery scales that seemed to sparkle with their own light. The cocoon had transformed him into a creature of both the land and the sea. On his back, a distinctive dorsal fin had grown and fin-like appendages emerged from his arms and legs. His skin, eye and hair color were transformed like a sea mammal's dark and light shades used for camouflage. He breathed naturally in his new element as the dolphins watched curiously. What was this thing? The dolphins darted under and around it. The boy turned and spun with equal ease. He seemed to have no problem among them. Where they went, he followed.

The leader of the pod clicked rapidly. He knew humans. They could be friend or foe. He had seen the wrecks of their ships that littered the sea bed, the product of their wars, and the great clouds of muck that floated from the mouths of their rivers. But this was something different. It seemed human, but no human could live in the sea. Already, it had the speed and agility of the fastest dolphin. Were there more? What could a fully grown one of its kind do? What could a thousand of its kind do? A trio of dolphins clicked at the leader. The creature should not live, they protested. It would bring harm. As they moved in to strike, the leader, a powerful dolphin named Cronos, hurled his body between the creature and the charging dolphins. "No!" he said. "The creature shall have his life. It is not a man." "It's worse!" the dolphins said. "You've seen what it can do, and it is just a child!"

Cronos held his position. He looked gravely at the creature. Perhaps they were right. If they waited too long, there could be no turning back. Again, he eyed the child, but rather than defiance, it merely smiled broadly. It had a curious twinkle in its eyes. Perhaps it's a sign from the Gods, Cronos thought. Why else would it have been left alone in the open sea? But he suspected that whatever this man-thing was or would be, it would certainly be something that all the creatures of the sea may one day come to fear or respect. "The tribe can decide," he said. "For now," said one of the trio, a husky dolphin named Gladiator. "But if he endangers the tribe, he dies." Cronos nodded, and the pod moved on.

As the dolphins surfaced for air, the winds above still howled. The great storm had slowed but had not ended. The tribe was accustomed to the strange goings on in the world above and sometimes below. Cronos had watched the lights in the sky descend over the years. But these were creatures of the surface. They were not his concern. He and his tribe were not alone in the Bermuda Triangle. Creatures large and small lived here. Humpback Whales, Giant Manta Rays, Sea Turtles, and Sharks. The dolphins and great whales had dominion, but that came because they respected the other creatures. Now, resting at the surface, the baby seemed at peace and began to respond to its strange traveling companions. The pod had many questions, but it was time for the dolphins to return to their tribe to share the news of the arrival of the new creature. Word had already begun to spread through the iconic shell telegraph about the baby human that swam like a dolphin and breathed like a fish.

The child was quickly taken to the tribe where it stirred as much curiosity as fear. The tribe knew the troubles that the humans had brought in the past. The elders had the scars to prove it. While the dolphins had coexisted with people, the elders were the ones with the greatest understanding of the damage that may still befall the ocean at the hand of the humans. As the ships above thundered in ever greater numbers across the shipping lanes, the dolphins had seen their food supplies shrink, the waters clouded and the ever present noise that followed them in even the deepest sea. The food supply was now being poisoned with tons of plastic and toxic waste that humans were carelessly dumping into the ocean. In recent years, loud sonic booms had caused mass strandings of whales and dolphins, killing thousands.

The tribe council assembled at the sea mount. It was a sacred place where important matters were often decided. By the time the elders arrived, Cronos could see great anxiety among the tribe. "What have you brought us, Cronos?" said the first elder. "A human? And how is this possible?" "It is clearly impossible," countered another elder.

The leader of the elders, a battle scarred female named Ereon, came forward. "Members of the tribe, fellow elders, we have all seen the creature. We know not what it is, but it clearly is not a human."

"It is worse," a dolphin said. "It is something in between. It will destroy us."

"We must kill it."

"Let it drown," said another. "Before it is too late."

A voice called out. "Wait," Cronos said, circling in. "Where is our compassion? These humans can be bad, yes, it has been proven true. But we must not judge them all. This baby may be something none of us can understand. But it also will not survive for long if we don't do something for it."

"Cronos, you are naïve," an elder said. "Your parents knew that the dolphins gave their trust to the humans long ago."

"… and we were hunted," Cronos said. "Yes, elder, I know the stories. I know the legends also say that a great leader will come and join us in our cause to save our mother ocean."

"Surely you are not implying …"

"Dear elder, I'm only saying that we dolphins have survived by our compassion for one another. Perhaps this strange child is not an omen, but a sign, a test. It swims, it breathes, it seems only to desire our love. I ask that that the tribe leave it under my care for now. I will watch it."

"And you will report to the council."

"Yes, of course."

The members of the council nodded solemnly.

"As you wish, Cronos. For now," Ereon said.

Cronos watched the tribe disassemble. He wondered what he had gotten himself into.

*Dolphin intelligence is alien, with brains the size of humans only 40 million years earlier...*

*W*

# CHAPTER THREE

# TRIBE

As the weeks passed, the duty of caring for the little creature was shared between Cronos and his sister Mara. Dolphins had many duties, but females often lead the tribe. Together, they tended to and fed the young creature, who seemed to have no shortage of desire to join the pod. But the entire pod had not accepted the creature yet. Cronos would lead it on short journeys through the calm, teal blue waters of the Caribbean where he could teach it their ways.

He taught it how to use the pod for protection, how the pod was a constantly moving world unto itself and how all must be sacrificed for the good of the pod. Many of the lessons the creature did not understand, and when it did not, Cronos would repeat the words sternly until finally giving in to his frustration, and letting the creature swim freely. As much as he disliked giving in, he was filled with wonder at the sight of the creature so at home in the water, perhaps even more so even than some dolphins. He watched as the creature dove and spun at incredible speed, racing up from the dark sea below and catapulting above the surface, sometimes as high as thirty feet in the air. And as always, he would splash back to the sea with a wide, ecstatic grin. Cronos had never seen such joy from a creature. When the time came for the creature to join the pod, Cronos felt a rush of anxiety. If the creature could not adapt, it would die. If it crossed one of the larger dolphins, it was still too small to defend itself. All it had now was its incredible speed and agility Cronos would see in short order how that alone would be more than enough to survive!

The first order of business for the dolphin tribe was the hunt. The pod moved as one along the edge of the coral reefs and the sandy ocean bottom in search of Spanish mackerel. Every spring, the mackerel returned to these waters and were a favorite food of the tribe. With their slender, bullet-shaped bodies, they sped through the water eluding even the fastest predators. The challenge of catching the mackerel only added to the challenge and the excitement for the tribe. From the rear of the pod, Cronos explained to the creature, who he had now taken to calling SeaWalker, that he thought he was a creature of both worlds. The world of the humans and the world of the sea. "Stay wide of the pod, SeaWalker, it is important for you to watch and learn." Then he directed the young creature's attention to the leaders who had begun to circle the fish, herding them, until the others of the pod could move into position. Quickly, one dolphin after another dove through the pod, emerging with a fish in their mouths.

SeaWalker did not wait. Immediately, he bolted toward the swirling commotion. Cronos tried to cut him off, but it was too late. In an instant, SeaWalker felt himself pummeled by thousands of fish. His body spun over and over against the flash of silver. His hands grabbed at the flurry of fish. But he caught nothing. By the time he opened his eyes, the mackerel and the pod had moved on, and SeaWalker was left staring into the face of a very angry Cronos. "When I tell you to do something, you must listen," Cronos fumed. "The ocean is a dangerous place. If you break the rules of the tribe, there is nothing I can do for you. Do you understand?" The child averted his eyes, then finally, he looked up ruefully, his deep blue eyes pooled with shame, and nodded.

There was so much to learn within the dolphin world beneath the waves, and SeaWalker had to learn fast if he was to survive. There were many dangers from sharks, killer whales and even the threat of other dolphin tribes. But, as Cronos reflected, he was reminded that the greatest danger of all came not from beneath the sea, but from the walkers above. It was getting worse during every full moon for each new generation. Killer nets covered much of the ocean, destroying fish, sharks, turtles and seabirds. In fact, many members of the dolphin tribes within the Bermuda Triangle had lost their lives to the ever-changing technology of the walkers. Almost all of the undersea families had been affected, and some nearly wiped out, by the ruthless, uncaring creatures that lived above. Sharks were dragged from their home by long lines with giant hooks, then pulled to the surface where humans cut off all their fins and horrifically threw them back into the sea to die a slow, painful death. Great clouds of poison and micro-plastics flowed from the mouths of their great rivers to the sea. But what could any of the dolphin tribes do against such might? Dolphins before him had tried. All had lost their lives. And what of the little creature, this SeaWalker, Cronos wondered? Dolphins believed in giving all creatures a chance to prove themselves. They thought that soon enough the true character of every creature would be known. But rather than the fear that humans caused, the little creature that seemed to love the ocean so much, it filled Cronos with a sense of wonder. As he watched SeaWalker, he knew instinctively that something had changed. It was in every particle of the water – and there would be no going back!

*Ancient tribes, dolphins and great whales, were here 50 million years before man...*

*W*

# CHAPTER FOUR

# SWIM ABOUT

After a restful evening lounging at the surface with Cronos, Mara and some of the other dolphins, SeaWalker decided to venture out into his new world. To the east, the light of the rising sun penetrated the surface as far as the eye could see. SeaWalker noticed the outlines of landmarks: a sea mount here, coral reefs there. He could see the commotion of the smaller creatures as they emerged from their protective covers. He took a moment to observe a hermit crab as it crawled along the sea floor. Its beady eyes followed SeaWalker's every move, until SeaWalker seized it in his webbed fingers for closer observation. The two locked eyes, trying to figure out the other's next intentions, until the hermit crab appeared to confirm that SeaWalker was no threat and resigned itself to hanging comfortably from SeaWalker's fingers for however long the experience might take.

SeaWalker thought the moment was as good as any to bring this new friend along with him. The crab didn't seem to mind and hung on tight to SeaWalker's fin as they bolted off to explore the morning. Everywhere he looked, SeaWalker saw something new to discover. Every rock he turned over revealed a world within a world. Every swaying piece of coral filled him with fascination.

# CHAPTER FOUR

As time passed, however, SeaWalker noticed a strange, persistent and very strange clicking around him. But the sound wasn't something he was hearing with his ears. It was as if it were coming from – or rather into his mind. He looked around, but the only animal close to him was the little hermit crab. SeaWalker closed his eyes. He formed a thought in his head and directed it at the crab.

Is that you making that racket?

SeaWalker received a very tiny, but distinctly clear answer in his mind, "Yes."

SeaWalker smiled. Things were certainly getting interesting. In fact, SeaWalker soon became keenly aware that the ocean was not a silent world at all, but rather a very noisy place. From his friend the crab crackling to other strange noises, the sea was alive with a symphony of music, color and light.

As time passed, SeaWalker grew strong, and most of the tribe had accepted him as one of its own. He became faster and more agile. His confidence grew. Best of all, his value to the pod was never higher. With his speed, he began to assist in herding the great schools of mackerel, darting into the blue, then twisting his body until the mackerel had no choice but to turn on themselves until they became a tighter and tighter ball of fish. From there, the members of the pod, old and young, could easily fill their stomachs.

Despite warnings from Cronos, SeaWalker began to venture further and further during his explorations, guided by his never-ending curiosity. "What is it you are looking for, SeaWalker?" Cronos had asked him once.

SeaWalker couldn't explain. Everything about the ocean fascinated him. But somewhere deep inside him, he remembered familiar voices speaking in a language he no longer knew. Perhaps, he thought, he could hear the voices again if he traveled far enough and he could discover what their words meant. By this time, Cronos, like an uneasy father, no longer tried to stop SeaWalker. He kept an eye on him as best he could, but with SeaWalker's great speed, watching him was not easy. With a mighty kick of his legs, SeaWalker could propel himself a mile away from the pod, and in the matter of an hour, he could be in an entirely new place altogether.

It was in these moments that SeaWalker would often find himself in strange, unfamiliar territory. Once, after a day of traveling, he discovered a giant undersea forest that covered much of the ocean from the floor to the surface. The swaying stalks beckoned

# CHAPTER FOUR

him to enter the canopy where the ocean's current pushed the forest this way and that. He swam through the thick kelp, his body swaying with the giant green branches and leaves. Nestled among the stalks, he came across a small, shy octopus. It had blended in so perfectly with its surroundings, it would have been easy to overlook. But by this time SeaWalker had developed a trained eye. Slowly, he reached out his hand. The octopus extended its tentacles, and they embraced. He could feel the soft suction of the animal's tentacles and admired its ability to reflect the ragged-edge texture of the kelp forest with its skin. Suddenly, the creature's skin changed and it jetted backward, leaving SeaWalker in a cloud of black ink and fog.

Something wasn't quite right. A dark shadow passed overhead, too fast for SeaWalker to see it. He sensed another presence, but the feeling quickly passed, and he decided to continue through the forest. As he entered the other side, he encountered a large group of black tip reef sharks engaged in an ancient mating dance. SeaWalker noticed small clouds of blood floating through the water. The mating rituals of sharks were very aggressive and sometimes the males bit the females for control. This in turn attracted the attention of a giant tiger shark that glided in with great stealth from the shadows and proceeded to circle the other sharks. In an instant, the massive tiger shark lunged and bit one of the black tip reef sharks in half, swallowing the middle section in one gulp. This was only the beginning. Soon, other tigers cruised in like battleships. One by one, they gorged on the smaller sharks. The sea was blood red in every direction. SeaWalker was in shock. He had taken part in countless hunts with the pod, but he had never witnessed anything like this. He was frozen stiff with fear and remained behind the large kelp forest canopy for several minutes when something poked him — and it nearly sent him shooting across the forest in fright! Fortunately, it wasn't a shark, but the crab who got scared and pinched him. When their eyes met, SeaWalker realized how scared the crab was and placed the tiny creature back on his dorsal fin as they turned and swam away at lightning speed from this strange and deadly place.

*Whales navigated the ocean planet for
fifty million years with an internal compass
known only to them...*

*W*

# CHAPTER FIVE

# FORBIDDEN SEA FOREST

The shark encounter left SeaWalker and his nervous hitchhiker in a state of panic. This forest under the sea seemed to go on forever. Strange sounds and shapes seemed to lurk behind every kelp bed, and the ever-changing cathedral of light filtering from above haunted him. SeaWalker heard the clicking of the crab in his mind. This place made the little creature nervous.

Sometimes, the imagination can be scarier than any reality. And SeaWalker certainly had a vivid imagination. Here, deep under the surface was a dense forest of giant kelp that could hide creatures, both real and imagined. He knew that sharks used the cover of the forest to kill its prey. His imagination was now in overdrive as he and his small companion raced through the giant kelp forest. His acute hearing allowed him to hear every noise and compounded the fear that something menacing might be stalking him. His heart was pounding as they continued to weave in and out of the trees. At one point, the sunlight above disappeared, and in the nearly black waters, all he could see were luminous, glowing eyeballs, which added to the fear that he was not alone not by any means.

# CHAPTER FIVE

The temperature was cold and SeaWalker, because of his anxiety, was freezing. Goosebumps covered his entire body as they continued their long journey back to the tribe.

Suddenly, something grabbed SeaWalker's ankle. Instinctively, he turned to free himself, but this only made the grip of whatever held him tighter. As he looked down, he saw he was completely entangled by the kelp and the more he struggled, the more entrapped he became. Panic set in. The kelp seemed to be a life form itself. The struggle left him exhausted. As he worked to calm himself, he saw an uproar in the distance. Something large was heading his way. Helpless and waiting for the worst, SeaWalker closed his eyes. When he finally summoned the courage to open them again, he was surrounded by members of his pod, led by Cronos, who tore away the entangling kelp from SeaWalker's legs.

The dolphins looked at him with puzzlement. SeaWalker turned away sheepishly.

"Listen, SeaWalker," Cronos said. "It is not safe for you to travel without your tribe. There are dangers here, many that you are not aware of. The risks are great, and unless you want to become part of the food chain, you will heed the advice of the elders. You must stay near the dolphin waters. Do you understand? We stay strong because of the group. We work together with intelligence and ancient wisdom of these waters." SeaWalker averted his eyes, "Yes."

SeaWalker could hear the clicking of the crab. It wanted to tell its side, but deep inside, it knew that they had been in great danger. One by one, the pod circled around SeaWalker. They led him and his friend away from the forbidden sea forest, back to the Triangle, where he would remain under their watchful protection... even if he didn't know it!

*The forbidden sea is only forbidden to those*
*who do not know her...*

*W*

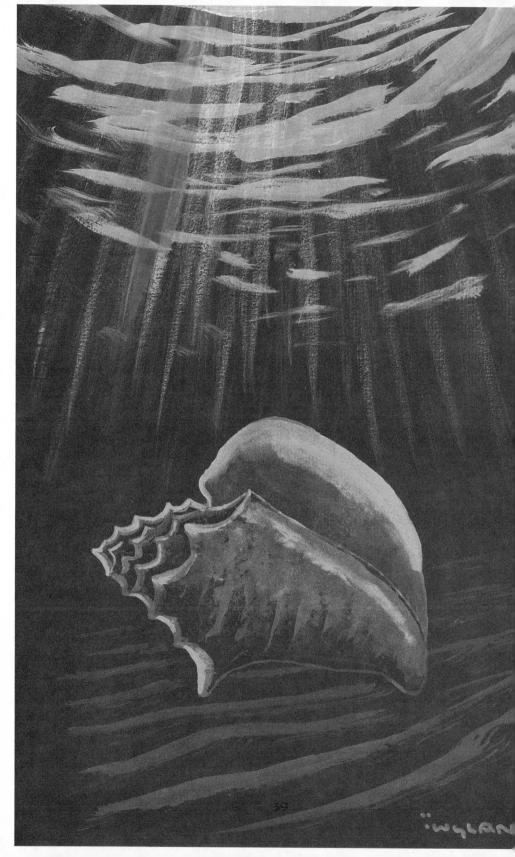

# CHAPTER SIX

# VOICES OF THE SEA

The next few weeks passed. Despite his yearning to explore, SeaWalker stayed close to the pod. He tried to heed the warnings of Cronos and the other dolphins. He knew they were right. When the pod was together, the pod was strong. But the call within him to discover the ocean grew stronger than ever. One night as the pod slept, SeaWalker awoke to the sound of a deep and distant rumbling, a sound that seemed to move through his very bones. He closed his eyes for a sense of where the sound might be coming from while stories of great giants told by his elders flashed back.

Whales have much larger brains than the humans above, they had explained. Orcas, who are the largest member of the dolphin family, also have larger brains, and both are considered much more intelligent. It's hard to measure because they have different kinds of intelligence, but clearly, humans could not last in the ocean for more than a few minutes. They are also more social than their human counterparts. The fact is that the humans, like the whales, evolved from the sea. Unfortunately, the humans have different DNA that gives them a sense of empowerment. They believe they preside over all life, and other animals are there just to serve them. The fact of the matter is that without the life-giving sea and the other animals, humans would go the way of the dinosaurs – extinct! All humans could leave the planet, and the planet would thrive, the elders explained. The whales have long exceeded the intelligence of the human species, but they never exploited it. They let the humans believe that they were the superior race. They must now decide whether to challenge the humans to ensure their survival. Before the humans even set foot on the land, the whales dominated their water world. For fifty million years, the whales thrived and understood that the balance of life depended on not destroying the environment. They also decided early on not to get into conflicts with the humans. Whales were thought of as peaceful, gentle beings that were there for man to use as they desired. Humans systematically slaughtered them since they found them, first near shore and then developing boats to hunt them at sea. The first commercial whaling expedition was in 1606 in Taiji, Japan. Today, it has expanded to giant commercial whaling fleets that indiscriminately hunt down these great whales in all parts of the ocean. With human technology, it seems the whales don't have a chance. Many have been hunted to extinction over the years.

Whale societies are extraordinarily complex with many generations living together. When one member is removed from the family, the entire tribe is threatened. To add insult to injury, not only have humans been slaughtering whales and dolphins, some are captured and kept in captivity for entertainment. Given a choice, most intelligent marine animals would rather perish first.

Far away, he saw in his mind an image of a dark place, deep and hidden, where dolphins never ventured. He saw strange twisting caves and huge, great moving shadows. The place called him. But what did it want? He couldn't leave the tribe again. Not now. But it was as if he had no choice. Finally, quietly, he slipped away into the night. He swam for hours, following the sound, until it was everywhere. As he descended deeper, he discovered a network of deep-sea canyons and caves like the ones he had seen in his mind. The voices were stronger now. He had no choice but to go forward.

The caves were ancient formations. Great undersea volcanoes had formed them. Upon closer inspection, these lava tubes were enormous, like great cathedrals of rock and glass. SeaWalker felt small and humbled, as if he were entering a place of great importance. The sound within the lava tube now seemed to be rising and falling. As he moved forward, he came to a great hall. Hundreds of great whales had amassed within the hall. The animals were not like anything he had ever seen. Each in itself seemed as big as SeaWalker's pod. With the flick of a tail, just

# CHAPTER SIX

one of these great creatures could easily destroy one of the great human ships above. Why had they gathered here? SeaWalker thought. The answer dawned on him slowly. This was some kind of meeting. But certainly like no meeting he had known. There was a sense of peace within the great hall, as if the animals were drawing their strength from the very sea itself and spreading this tranquility through their collective voice to all creatures large and small, near and far. The voice they transmitted carried with it a message. Something was happening in the ocean. The voice didn't say what.

Then, another presence seemed to enter SeaWalker's mind. It spoke to him calmly

"You are welcome here SeaWalker," the new voice said. "Please do not be afraid."

SeaWalker turned.

"Who is this?" he asked.

"Who is not important," the voice responded. "What is happening here?"

"There is a great disturbance in the ocean. A disruption of the balance of our sacred world." Before SeaWalker could respond, the voice continued. "Restoring this balance is a cause of great concern to our kind. It is why we have gathered here, as we have done in times of great crisis for millions of years. Our legends have foretold of one who will join our effort to save this world. He will be neither of the sea or the land, but one of both worlds." SeaWalker shook his head. The voice couldn't possibly mean him, but in his bones he new knew otherwise.

"What can I do?"

"It is not your time yet." "Why was I brought here?"

"There will be a time when we shall call you. The time is soon." SeaWalker had so many questions, but the voice had stopped. He scanned the great hall. The whales continued in their repose within the great cathedral. At least they had given him a clue. He had sensed it earlier, but now he knew.

Then, SeaWalker felt a tingling sensation, a familiar feeling crawling up his back. Suddenly, a tiny voice popped into his head. Wow, Wow, Wow, the voice said. SeaWalker turned and realized it was his tiny friend, the crab, who had been with him the whole time and was silently speaking with him, just like the whales had. SeaWalker smiled at his friend as they turned to leave the lava tubes. But now he felt the force of something heavy weighing on him. Something he could not escape.

*Cetaceans live in a sea of sound...*

*W*

# CHAPTER SEVEN

# AWAKENING

**S**eaWalker rejoined the tribe before dawn. Neither Cronos nor any of the others noticed that he had been gone. He tried to close his eyes but all he could see was the strange hall within the great lava tube. His mind raced. It had felt like a dream. Was it real? Other voices filled his head. He seemed unable to turn them off. The thoughts of dolphins around him came at him from every direction. And not only from the dolphins, but other animals as well: the worry of a flounder buried beneath the surface of the sand, with only its eyeballs visible, nervously hiding from predators; a giant stingray gliding overhead; a great hammerhead shark searching for something to fill its empty stomach. Large and small, every creature expressed itself. Whatever fear or worry, anger or concern, SeaWalker seemed to hear it all. His mind cried out in pain. His love for the tribe had grown each day. He knew he had failed them time and again, but he also knew that he would die for his friends. He would do everything in his power to ensure the safety of the tribe.

His awakening consumed every molecule in his body. He achieved the highest level of consciousness and beyond-both human and cetacean. He also felt more powerful in every way.

# CHAPTER SEVEN

His mind, body and spirit were ready to take on whatever challenges he and his family would surely encounter, now and in the future. For now, it was bliss. Everything came into clear focus, and he began to not only understand his place in the tribe, but in the Universe. The powers bestowed on him would be used for good and also allow him to take on the evil that seemed to permeate both the above and below worlds. His dolphin family knew instinctively that he was pure and now ready to join them as they looked to a future that was far more dangerous because of the walkers. He felt a deep sense of enlightenment that seemed to be there from the beginning but now was in his new DNA and in every fiber of his existence.

As his thoughts flowed, great and powerful, a shudder seemed to run through the tribe. All of the dolphins around him jolted awake. Many looked at each other, then they turned to SeaWalker. In a moment, SeaWalker was surrounded by scores of dolphins, led by Cronos.

"So it is true," Cronos said.

SeaWalker was confused, "I do not understand."

"We have heard you SeaWalker," Cronos said. He gestured to the other dolphins. "All great cetaceans possess the voice of the sea.

It is what binds our tribe and others. How long have you known this?"

SeaWalker did not know what to say. Was it possible that his thoughts had reached the tribe?

"In moments of great need, the voice allows us to share with our brothers and sisters. Your need reached us. Your truth was known to us. This is a great moment for you and the tribe. For you are now truly one of us."

That evening, there was a great celebration. SeaWalker was granted the lead in his first hunt with the pod. As he swam to the front of the pod, he could see the faces of all the dolphins he had come to know over the years: the families he had grown with, the tribal elders and the fearsome hunters. All, it seemed, were here for this passing ritual. Cronos and Magda escorted him to the lead. The pod began to pick up speed, and with a great kick of his mighty legs, SeaWalker led the pod on an unforgettable hunt. For the first time, he felt as if he truly belonged.

*Dolphins live in peace, only taking
what they need to ensure the environment
and other species survive...*

*W*

# CHAPTER EIGHT

# WHALE RIDER

SeaWalker had traveled to many places. He had seen underwater volcanoes and great kelp forests. He saw massive, mid-ocean atolls. But he had never seen anything like the strange, blue island before him that rose and vanished, then rose again. With his curiosity aroused, he swam toward the landmark, looking for signs of life along its smooth, shiny surface. But no matter how far he went, the island stayed the same size. He sped up, thinking perhaps now it would be closer, but again, there was no change. He took a deep breath and then bolted with a kick of his legs. He swam and swam, only to find himself treading empty water. The mysterious island was nowhere to be seen. Moments later, he was shocked to see the island beneath his webbed feet. It rose rapidly, lifting him high above the surface, then began to move forward at an enormous speed. SeaWalker had no idea what to make of this phenomenon. The island plowed into the water, leaving a great wake behind it. Then with a loud rumble, a giant spray of water erupted beneath SeaWalker's feet, lifting him even higher in the sky.

The spray stopped suddenly, and he was pulled back with a thump to the moving island. When the island began to sink again, SeaWalker decided to hang on to see where it would take him. Down they went. Then a voice came into his head: "Are you the SeaWalker I have heard of, the one the great whale elders spoke of?"

SeaWalker had no idea how to respond. "I guess so," he said. "Who are you?"

"My name is Blue," the voice answered. "And I have lived in these waters for over two hundred years. The first hundred, they harpooned us. My kind became few. The second hundred, they poisoned my home and used their great ships to drag the sea of my food." Then Blue asked, "Are you one of them?"

SeaWalker hesitated. "I'm not sure," he said. "But I would like to help you if I can."

"You can start by getting off my back, young one, and coming around front so I can see you," the whale said.

SeaWalker did as Blue asked. He found himself eye to eye with an ancient, soulful creature whose face confirmed the stories of loss and great change that Blue had hinted at. Blue's eye was nearly half the size of SeaWalker, and to his wonder, the whale's body seemed to go on forever, eventually disappearing into the far off distance.

"Indeed, you are strange," Blue said. "You look almost like a human, but clearly you are of the sea. You have fins, gills and the skin of the fastest sea creatures." He stopped. "Tell me, how is such a thing possible?"

SeaWalker couldn't answer. "I don't know why I'm here. I was found by the dolphin tribe."

Blue sniffed. "The dolphins, hmm?"

"Yes."
Blue's voice grew quiet.

"Then it is destiny," Blue said. He eyed SeaWalker again, as if he had made a great consideration and approved. "But enough of this. I must eat. I must reach the plankton breeding grounds soon."

"Well, Blue,' SeaWalker said. "If it's all the same to you, I'd love to go with you and hear more about your past. Maybe I can try some plankton too!" Blue nodded agreeably and led SeaWalker to a murky field of water that flickered with giant clouds imperceptible movement. Blue forged his way through the field, taking massive amounts of water into his cavernous mouth in a single gulp. The scope of it amazed SeaWalker, who hovered at a safe distance to avoid accidentally colliding with the great whale.

As the day wore on, in between feeding, Blue shared stories of the sea with SeaWalker that had been passed down from his grandfather to his father and finally to him. His descendants had roamed the oceans for millions of years and only in the last century had they been threatened by man. Before that time, the whale had no natural enemies. Now, their numbers had diminished. And it was whispered that the time of the whales would soon be over. Blue explained to SeaWalker that although the Blues were the largest cetaceans, they were by no means the only ones out there. Some, like the vaquita, were no larger than SeaWalker. While others, like the sperm whale, were giants and had huge teeth, unlike Blue who strained the food from the sea using plates of baleen.

As Blue dove into the krill, SeaWalker marveled at how the largest animal in the ocean could survive by eating only the smallest creatures. These tiny krill and plankton were clearly a delicacy for the whale, and Blue swallowed them by the ton. Again and again, Blue lunged at the clouds of krill, inhaling more food than SeaWalker would have ever thought possible, his belly swelling to unimaginable proportions. At one point, Blue began to eat with such a frenzy that he seemed to forget all about SeaWalker, who was lost in a cloud of plankton and was sucked up into Blue's mouth along with the mounds of krill.

SeaWalker found himself in the dark, his body turning end over end and smashing against the long fringes of baleen that draped from the top of the great whale's mouth. Suddenly, Blue's massive tongue pressed against the baleen and pushed out the water, leaving behind only the krill, then sweeping the krill into his stomach. If SeaWalker didn't act fast, he would soon be little more than a side dish with the krill. He tried to communicate with the whale, using the voice in his mind, but it was clear that the only interest Blue had was feeding. Finally, with a powerful burst, SeaWalker flung himself against the front of the whale's mouth. Blue shuddered, then relented. When he finally opened his mouth, SeaWalker rolled out, sputtering, and out of breath. "Was that you in there, little one?" Blue said.

SeaWalker tried to catch his breath. "You couldn't tell? I could have died in there."

"Impossible," Blue said.

"What?" SeaWalker cried. "Of course it was possible."

"No, SeaWalker. If I had swallowed you, there would have been a simple solution."

SeaWalker shook his head. He was clearly flustered, but he was also curious. "And what would that have been?"

"Easy," Blue said. "You could have simply swam around until you got pooped out."

SeaWalker stared at this great, wise whale in disbelief. Blue remained motionless, then moments later, roared with laughter. SeaWalker's pride gave way, and soon, both of them were laughing uncontrollably. For SeaWalker, he had experienced what he would come to know as his very first joke.

*No other creature on the planet has adapted to
their environment like whales...*

*W*

# CHAPTER NINE

# REVELATIONS

The stench of Blue's smelly mouth followed SeaWalker on his long journey back to the pod. His long, green - and now green and orange - hair hung in clumps. He had to stop several times to remove a wriggling a piece of dead krill. He'd had enough excitement for one day, that was certain. Maybe all of this adventure was overrated. When he got home, he told himself that he would sleep. At the thought of reaching the pod, he swam faster, slicing through the water and periodically bursting through the surface porpoising in a long arc, then submerging again. He noticed on one of these leaps that storm clouds were assembling fast on the horizon. The clouds were dark and towering, and he could see flashes of lightning flicker from one cloud to the next. He was told that lightning was just God moving furniture. The wind rose, and the waves began to swell higher until they too were crashing into one another. SeaWalker charged forward. He had seen many storms before. With his speed, he could usually outrun them.

As the storm closed in, the sound of thunder boomed across the sky. The explosions rattled SeaWalker's very bones. His skin flowed with energy. It was as if the entire world had been shaken,

# CHAPTER NINE

then turned upside down. SeaWalker felt alive, like never before. With each burst of lightning, he began to see visions: A hazy image of a storm-tossed sailboat fighting desperately against the ravages of a hurricane. Two humans, panicked, and speaking in words he did not understand. They were in a terrible state of fear, but not for themselves. He heard the name Walker, and he realized that somehow they were talking about him. But how? Who were these people? SeaWalker felt a great despair overcome him. Faster, he swam, his body a powerful hammer against the waves. With each kick, he summoned more strength, urging his body on, to go faster and faster, to get home. He did not want to think about storms and sailboats and humans he did not know. His home was near, and he would be there soon.

The storm, however, continued to grow. The waves pushed higher. SeaWalker fought for every inch he could in order to move forward. Threads of lights raced across the sky, each with its own explosion of thunder. The clouds were moving at such a speed now that they seemed to gather into shapes of land and sea. In one mighty collision of clouds, the shape of an ancient human formed. However, SeaWalker sensed something different about this human. Unlike the reckless humans of the stories he had heard, he felt himself in the presence of a great spirit that lived in a quiet place in harmony with the land, just as the dolphins and the whales did in the sea. How could this be? SeaWalker thought.

# REVELATIONS

More visions flashed through SeaWalker's mind: Peaceful tribes of humans who took only what they needed from the land and sea, whose numbers had fallen like the whales. Wars and destruction and the peaceful tribes disappearing.

It seemed he was now in an altered state, and the images kept coming in vivid color. It seemed as if his short life was racing through his mind like a movie, but it was real! Maybe the Universe was trying to tell him something. A higher power now consumed him on a spiritual level, and all his senses were in full development bringing wisdom that would serve him well in the future. His knowledge was accelerating at breakneck speed, underscoring his unique ability to absorb information like no being, past or present. He was absorbing all this amazing information and finally beginning to understand his place in the universe.

SeaWalker had an awakening. Again, he remembered the words of the great whales. "You are of the land and the sea, part of both worlds," they had told him. It was then he knew. It was the reason why the sea called him to adventure. He was to learn everything from the kingdom below in order to one day enlighten human kind about the preservation of both worlds. The vision of the clouds showed him that the way would be perilous. A war was looming, and SeaWalker might not survive. But he knew he had to try. He knew that if he didn't succeed, the fate of the planet was at stake. The planet could move toward the light of harmony, and it would prosper. Or it could be plunged into darkness.

The storm had awakened him. When it was over, the clouds opened up to a starry night. Suddenly, a shooting star, the largest he had ever seen, raced across the sky and landed with a great spray of water less than a mile away. It was close enough for SeaWalker to explore.

*Dolphin societies are complex with many generations living at the same time, passing on the knowledge of their ancestors...*

*W*

# CHAPTER TEN

# ATLANTIS FOUND

**S**eaWalker raced to the location of the fallen meteor. When he arrived, he could still see a ring of water from the meteor's impact. Strange things often happened in the Bermuda Triangle. Bizarre weather and things falling from the sky were not as unusual as one might think. And yet, even in a place such as this, there was something about this rock from the sky that called out for his attention.

Cronos had told him of the massive warships that crossed most of the Bermuda Triangle. These ships were often ablaze in light throughout the evenings as they lowered special ships that disappeared into the water and re-emerged hours later. It seemed the humans were searching for answers to their own mysteries. But SeaWalker sensed that they didn't share his interest in the well-being of the sea or its inhabitants.

The water where the meteor had crashed was eerily calm. SeaWalker could hear his own breathing amid the quiet as he swam ever deeper. He could feel the pressure against his temples and realized he had gone far beyond the depth limits of any dolphin. Deeper still he went, plunging into near total darkness

# CHAPTER TEN

until he noticed a faint aura of blue light in the distance below. It wasn't like any surface light he knew, and it grew brighter as he approached. Perhaps it was some type of celestial light from the meteor or the very bottom of the sea was infused with some kind of bioluminescence? Against the light, he began to see remnants of a lost city. Marble pillars in ruins and cathedrals of stone.

Could this be the lost civilization of Atlantis that descended from Greek mythology? A civilization with technology beyond its time? The lost empire was thought to be a myth. But was SeaWalker entering the now submerged city that was part of the mysterious Bermuda Triangle? Whatever this was, it had energy and was drawing SeaWalker into its gravitational force.

Far from feeling his usual elation of discovery, an other worldly feeling crept over him as he entered what he discovered to be an entire city that had been lost for generations. He glided overhead at a safe distance. The city seemed to go on forever. He swam in for closer inspection. Whoever inhabited the city was incredibly advanced. There were great boulevards and markets and elegant marble buildings, and SeaWalker wondered what could possibly have brought about the destruction of such a magnificent city. Strewn across the sea floor were enormous obelisks with strange writings. Perhaps it was a clue, he thought. He was lost in thought when, from the corner of his eye, he saw an apparition flying through the corridors beside him. The hair on the back of his neck stood up when something bumped into him. SeaWalker jumped in surprise. "Gotcha!" a voice said.

SeaWalker sputtered and found himself looking directly into the face of Finn, a young dolphin from one of the local tribes. Like SeaWalker, Finn was always finding himself in trouble, much to the chagrin of the his tribe's elders. So, it came as no surprise that Finn was beside SeaWalker now. "You're not supposed to be here dude," said Finn.

"I know I'm not supposed to be here," said SeaWalker. "My question is how are you able to withstand the pressure here? Not to mention this place is just plain creepy."

"Alright, you caught me," Finn said. "It's a little trick I picked up from the elders in my tribe. A lot of practice, and I've been able to go deeper than almost any dolphin I know. I've been coming here for the last couple of years. In fact, follow me, I want to show you something."

They moved through the lost city, to a cornerstone engraved in marble. "What's it say?" SeaWalker asked.
Finn whispered, "Atlantis."

# CHAPTER TEN

Seeing the empty expression on SeaWalker's face, Finn explained that SeaWalker had stumbled upon the lost city described in Greek mythology.

"And now we know where it is," Finn said proudly. As Finn spoke, another shadow in the distance darted behind a building.

"Did you see that?" SeaWalker said. Finn turned.
SeaWalker pointed, "Over there!"

Soon, he saw more willowy, human-like creatures passing through the streets and dilapidated buildings.

Seeing this lost city was amazing and strange. The marble structures looked like they were ancient, but many were broken as if there was a large earthquake. Looking through one of the giant structures, SeaWalker even glanced at a large silver saucer that seem to have crashed into the seafloor. Near the saucer, there seemed to be a number of apparitions - ghost-like, human-like forms with big heads. Like the saucer, they seemed to be silver but also translucent. There was a lot of debris including human skulls littering the seafloor. It was really creepy and made SeaWalker nervous.

Finn nodded. His voice drew to a whisper. "That's the weirdest part. As near as I can tell, they're lost souls - ghosts," he explained.

"So far, they're harmless. Most are shy, really shy. I once overhead the elders talk about a place in the Triangle where lost creatures are caught between the worlds of life and death, and I think this is it. I think that's why no one comes here." His eyes followed a ghost in a blue hat carrying a fishing pole. "They seem to be going about their lives, over and over and over."

"Do they know they're dead?" SeaWalker asked.

Finn shrugged, "I don't know. Maybe. But if they do, they don't seem to mind. But that's not all. This place gets even stranger. Check this out." He led SeaWalker through the corridors of the lost city, until they came to a large arena where thousands of the ghosts packed the seats. SeaWalker marveled at the range of clothing on each of the apparitions. He recognized some of the clothes from his observations of the humans. There were sailors and pilots, along with tourists in brightly colored shirts with leaping marlins and still others in sandals with black socks. Hundreds more wore every manner of hats and sunglasses and carried fishing poles. All were in a zombie-like state. Like the city itself, they all seemed lost and frozen in the time.

As they swam past the arena, SeaWalker noticed a faint light.

# CHAPTER TEN

"Over there, Finn!"

SeaWalker raced toward the source of the light. It soon became clear that it was not a single light at all but rather a series of lights that stretched for nearly a mile along a stretch of sandy road.

"Yes, I've seen it," Finn said. "But I've been too afraid to approach it."

At that moment, a silver saucer-shaped object careened into view, hovering over the undersea road, then proceeded more slowly along the lighted pathway until it disappeared into the distance. SeaWalker had never seen anything like it. Then, from the darkness, a strange group of figures approached. They were nothing like the apparitions in the arena. They had white, gray and green phosphorescent skin and floated effortlessly over the road… They must be aliens! SeaWalker counted at least six of them, followed by a much taller entity that shadowed the group. Next to them, in a strange moving, cocoon-like bubble, SeaWalker saw a man and woman in Bermuda shorts and matching blue shirts. The man was wearing a woven palm hat and sunglasses, and both of them had cameras around their necks, as if they had just been snatched from the surface. Finn grabbed SeaWalker, "Don't let them see us."

As they hid behind a cluster of buildings, they watched as the aliens were greeted by more of their kind. "Bizarre," said Finn.

*We now know something is out there...*

W

# CHAPTER ELEVEN

# DEEP SECRET

Atlantis, according to folklore, sank beneath the sea after a massive earthquake and volcano eruption. SeaWalker was mesmerized by what he saw. In ancient times, this must've been an amazing, vibrant city, but sadly, the ruins are now home to what appear to be ghostly souls walking around in an altered state. Even worse, they were being controlled by alien forces. Once one of the richest cities, it was now a graveyard of buildings occupied by lost souls wandering around hopelessly and being used as food by their alien abductors. Judging by some of the ghostly characters, the aliens had used this area to harvest the walking dead, for generations. Ghoulish didn't begin to describe the nightmare occupied the once vibrant minds of the men and women who never saw this coming. The long history of ships and planes mysteriously disappearing into the Bermuda Triangle now seemed to be a reality as SeaWalker couldn't believe his eyes.

SeaWalker and Finn watched as the flying saucer beings took the man and woman in the cocoon to a weird machine with a green light that moved back and forth over the couple. When the aliens turned off the machine, the cocoon disappeared and the man and woman sat up with the same ghostly appearance as the other zombie-like creatures floating around the city.

"What are they doing?" SeaWalker said.

"I'm not sure, but I think those aliens are bringing the people down here," Finn responded. "Somehow they're using the energy of the people for food. Maybe that's what the machine was for. They use them little by little, then hold them here until they're ready to use them again."

Moments later, the aliens led the new arrivals down the main road to the arena, still followed by the larger entity that Finn called, "The Boss." As the group made its way through the corridors, all of the ghost zombies that had been floating nearby suddenly froze and bowed in the direction of The Boss. SeaWalker could feel something tug on his mind, too. His resistance seemed to catch the attention of The Boss who looked in their direction and scowled for a moment before continuing forward. When the aliens arrived at the front of the arena, the man and woman were added to a small group of new lost souls that were already there. In his mind, SeaWalker could hear the voice of The Boss addressing the new group. "Welcome humans," he said. "Congratulations on your arrival. You have been chosen for a great journey. There is no need to be afraid. Soon you will travel to a faraway place where your souls will be released from the bonds of earth, and you will live forever. Behold!"

He lifted his arms just as a huge flying saucer floated into view above them. Then, one by one, he touched each of the zombies who rose and floated towards the vessel. As the last zombie entered, SeaWalker and Finn noted the look of fear that had taken over the zombie's face. But SeaWalker wasn't able to look for long. An alien abruptly shut the door, and the vessel sprang upward, disappearing toward the surface.

With the aliens gone, the zombies resumed their movements as if nothing had happened.

"What does it mean?" Finn said.

"You tell me," SeaWalker said. "It's giving me the creeps. Let's get the heck out of here!" As he turned, he ran into a ghostly old sea Captain with a red beard and paper white skin. As soon as their eyes met, the Captain spoke. "I have been here for 742 years,". "And each night they come and leave with some of our mates."

"But why?" SeaWalker asked.

"No one knows," the old man replied. "You see, no one has ever returned from the spaceship. We can only wait for someone to save us. But I fear that will never happen."

SeaWalker learned that the Captain was actually a Viking who once sailed the North Sea in search of new worlds. He had been a great leader, but his crew had been taken over the years by the aliens. "I am the last of my kind," he said sadly. "Please help me."

"We would like to help you," Finn said. "But we can't stay here much longer. It's only a matter of time before the aliens catch us. But we promise to come back. We promise."

The Captain nodded, "Very well."

As they swam away, SeaWalker looked back. "Don't forget us," the Captain pleaded. "Remember, our world is your world. It's only a matter of time before they come for you too."

He repeated the words over and over again as Finn and SeaWalker quickly disappeared, swimming as fast as they could for home.

*Aliens have long been part of our planet,*
*living in the sea ...*

*W*

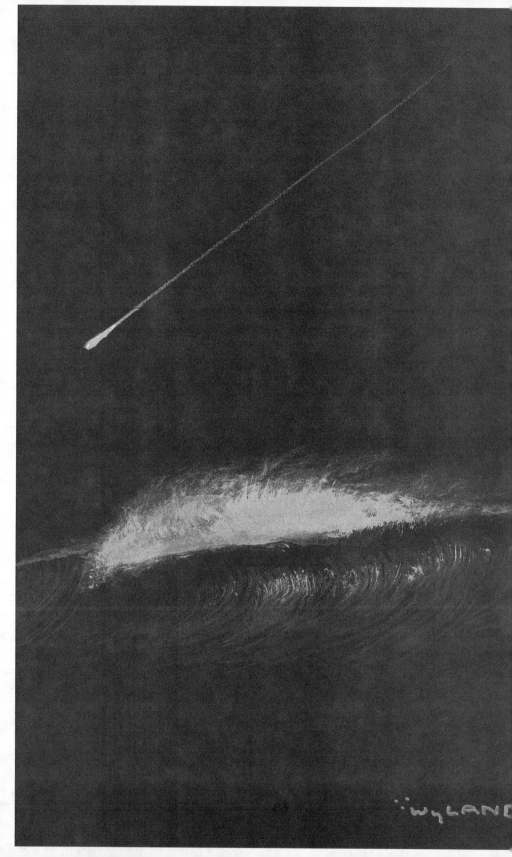

# CHAPTER TWELVE

# DRIVEN

**S**ome things you can't un-see. Gross, mutilated zombies are at the top of the list. The living dead roamed around Atlantis like ghosts floating in the Dead Sea. Whatever happened here, stayed here, except for the poor souls that were beamed up to saucers and taken to other worldly places for God knows what. It's hard to feel sorry for the Walkers knowing how they continue to plunder the ocean with no regard for the health of the planet. Still, SeaWalker had compassion from both his human heritage and from dolphins. He sees how these poor people have been held captive. It was beyond sad, and both SeaWalker and Finn couldn't help but feel bad for these tortured humans. They never saw it coming, whether being pulled into the abyss from the force of the Bermuda Triangle or being abducted from other parts of the planet. Somehow they ended up here in an eternal living nightmare.

Both SeaWalker and Finn were creeped out by the encounter they experienced while seeing Atlantis firsthand. It was a long swim back to the tribe.

# CHAPTER TWELVE

"What did he mean when he said, 'Our world is your world?'" Finn asked.

SeaWalker shrugged. "I don't know, Finn. But we have to do something. We have to help them."

"But they're humans..."

"They were humans," SeaWalker said.

The old Captain's words lingered. It was no accident that SeaWalker had found that place. He was always stumbling across places and things that revealed new things to him. There was something familiar about the strange bubble that the man and the woman were in. Where had SeaWalker seen it before? The long trip back gave him time to think.

He realized he was quite different from the other members of his dolphin family. If not for them, he would have surely died. Quite different indeed, he loved them and he enjoyed the time that they took with him to share their knowledge and wisdom. He had a moment of clarity when he realized that everything was happening for a reason. He felt compelled to absorb every moment and had a desire to contribute not only to the tribe, but to all the animals in the sea, from the largest whales to the smallest crustaceans, like his little friend the crab. He realized each of them had a role to play in the secret balance that kept the sea alive for millions and millions of years. The sea that was his home was a continuing story of fascinating creatures. The above world was beautiful too, as he loved the sunrises over the Triangle, and when the full moon would rise and when the oceans would become even more active when the luminous light would penetrate the surface. Once in a while, he would see a million shooting stars, some landing very close. Sometimes, he would even make a wish on a star. He wished he knew from where he came. He had these feelings, but he couldn't really understand them just yet. He felt that somehow he was connected to the above world... the air, the land and the whole Universe. But for now, he wanted to prove that he was worthy of the respect of his dolphin tribe family. He wanted to prove that he could join them in their rituals. And that he could compete with them in the ways of their ancestors. SeaWalker and Finn continued their long journey back to home base – and they didn't really have a whole lot to say. Both felt stunned by what they had seen, by what they had experienced. It was strange, and they didn't want to talk about it. Not now, maybe not for a very long time. One thing was for sure, they had somehow seen something strange and amazing, they knew that one day they would have to return and deal with it. After all, they had promised to go back and help the lost souls. For now, they swam at a good speed, and the ocean went from blue water deserts of open ocean to dramatic coral formations... undersea architecture, some more sophisticated and larger than anything on land. The coral reefs were still evolving after millions of years. Giant elkhorn corals reached upward like giant fingers toward the surface. Brain corals of every size and formation dotted the seascape. Beautiful purple sea fans swayed among the gentle currents along with soft corals of every imaginable color from pinks to greens of every shade. The oceans undersea garden was radiant! All of it alive, and throughout the coral, a multitude of colorful reef fish and other animals – thousands of them - each with their own personality and characteristics, going about their day to day business of survival. Each knowing that they are a different rung in the food chain. It was an amazing time to be alive. Imaging the past, the present and even looking to the future, for a moment, they forgot about the lost souls. There was so much knowledge, so much to learn, so much to do. SeaWalker was like a sea sponge, absorbing all the elements that his senses could handle. He could hear the echoes, the chatter and all the animals communicating. He realized that he was special in some way. That he had a gift, and he wanted to use it for good - not only for his own family... for all the members of his ocean family. He was thirsty for more information and knowledge, and he began to believe that he was there to make a difference. He was at that place, at that moment, to do something great! It was an incredible moment of clarity for him. He was driven to find out why.

*Man has always been driven to destroy
what they don't understand...*

*W*

# CHAPTER THIRTEEN

# END OF THE PLANET

O ne morning as the first light pierced the warm tropical waters of the Triangle, SeaWalker was awakened with a vision that was pulling him towards the light, heading east. He did not know why he was being pulled like a magnet. Even the ocean currents were pushing him towards destinations unknown. In fact, the currents were getting stronger, and he was now being pushed through the water at a dizzying rate. He soon realized he was stuck to the Gulf Stream, the conveyor belt of the sea. After several hours that seemed like minutes, he saw what appeared to be a mirage on the horizon. Could it be the end of the planet? He had heard tales of such a myth, but they were never considered to be true. As he finally reached the edge, just below the surface, the water cascaded like a giant waterfall, and it stretched as far as the eye could see in both directions. Then suddenly he realized he was being forced over the edge of the blue planet. He tried to kick against the force to no avail. He tumbled over the edge and felt the gravitational pull as he headed straight down towards the core of the earth. Now, he was tumbling out of control, with no sense of direction for what seemed like an eternity. SeaWalker then plummeted into boiling hot water that was void of all life. The steamy water smelled toxic, and the color was rusty brown, gray and black and as thick as blood. All around him, objects whizzed by like shooting stars in the sky, things not of the ocean, but of the land. Manmade things, many things he had never seen, but knew instinctively. From tires to barrels of toxic waste, eroded and leaking, even refrigerators. It was the largest garbage dump anyone or anything could imagine. For decades, people had been using the oceans as a toilet – and this is where it got flushed. Piled miles high, in all directions, all brought to this place by the Gulf Stream - the ocean's conveyor belt that collects all of the trash from land and ships. Indeed, it looked like the end of the world – the dead world. Nothing could live here. SeaWalker was beginning to feel ill and started coughing. Unfortunately, he inhaled some of the toxic waters and debris and began chumming uncontrollably. His only chance was to make a swim for it, holding one hand over his mouth and nose. He made a run for the surface and was suddenly clobbered by a computer monitor, nearly knocking him unconscious. Faster and faster, the debris came: pots, chemicals, plastic bottles, tires, faster than he could overcome them. Cigarette butts stung his flesh like jellyfish tentacles. Nearly overwhelmed and exhausted, he finally saw a small speck of light through the debris, a mile or more from the surface. Swim! he told himself. He was covered with a green and black goo created from hazardous waste materials, It slowed his momentum. But worse was his mind. It raced. What could this place be? Where there was no life, no life giving oxygen, where all the trash of the world landed, where there was nothing but discarded, dead things. Then suddenly something grabbed his leg.

He was afraid to look, but he had to! This place wasn't completely dead after all. Something existed. A horrible mutation, an animal from the past primordial seas, a grotesque monster that perhaps had once been like him but was now horribly misshapen and ten times its former size. This four-eyed creature of the deep seemed to evolve from pure chemical waste, with primeval instincts. It made no noise. In fact, it had no visible mouth. It merely swam and engulfed its prey, absorbing it into its toxic body, sucking the life force from its quarry. And now he was the prey. SeaWalker kicked furiously, making a desperate motion and a 360-degree spin in order to escape its all encompassing grasp as he raced toward the surface.

What the hell was that, SeaWalker wondered.

The encounter helped to clean off a lot of the toxic waste from SeaWalker's body. As he swiftly swam away, he decided to look over his shoulder to see if he could see the creepy beast, it headed back towards the toxic wasteland where its was quickly eaten by another, even larger, monster! It was absorbed into the darkness back with a slurping sound. SeaWalker reached the surface just in time to gasp for fresh air, and he continued to move away from the area that he would call the Deep Waste Sea. It was a long swim back against the raging current. Luckily, he was able to hitch a ride with a school of blue fin tuna, drafting in their wake. SeaWalker had a symbiotic relationship with the tuna and all large apex predators. Blue fins grew up to twelve feet long and weighed hundreds of pounds. They were fast, powerful swimmers. He certainly didn't have a symbiotic relationship with that thing that had just tried to absorb him. He had never seen anything like it. And hoped never to see it again. After many hours, he arrived back home in the Triangle, where he shared his awful encounter with many of the elders. They had heard stories of this place from the time human civilization began. They had always stayed away. They had always been curious and now had a first hand account of what the end of the underworld looked like. They were sure they never wanted to visit, and were happy that SeaWalker survived this perilous journey. They warned him to never again attempt such a dangerous trip, alone and unaided. SeaWalker gave his word that he had no intention of going back to that awful, deadly place.

*In the end, the planet will survive without man...*

*W*

# CHAPTER FOURTEEN

# OCEAN WARRIOR

It was several days before SeaWalker felt like his old self. The toxic sea had taken a lot of his energy, and he developed a severe infection. Unconscious for nearly four days, he awoke to find several of the elders applying natural medicines from the deep water. The encounter had left him weak and barely alive. But SeaWalker was strong, and his will to live overcame the forces that threatened to overcome him. Each day he became stronger, drinking fish oil and taking vitamins derived from the bounty of the sea. This gave SeaWalker much time to think about his purpose. He was determined to be an ocean warrior, fighting for the protection of his friends in the sea and the protection of the waters that were vital to all species. He vowed to protect the oceans and continue to gain knowledge. He realized that he must somehow begin his learning of the above world if he were to help save the sea. This was a big risk for not only SeaWalker but all ocean inhabitants. The humans above had only left the sea some four million years ago. Evolving from wriggling sea creatures to the lands dominate species. But SeaWalker's natural curiosity led him to the conclusion that he must somehow find his way to the shore and begin the process of connecting human minds to the minds in the water. His biggest challenge came from both sides. The ocean beings and the humans had a long history of distrust and broken treaties. Only a few of the native people of the above world seemed to appreciate the balance that had to be protected to ensure that the sea survived, not only for the fish and aquatic animals but for all mankind. Maybe that was the answer. Find the last remaining native tribes in the above world and begin a dialogue to bridge the two worlds. At the same time, he realized that he had to begin to convince the tribe elders of his intentions. This was a great risk he was taking. The humans could use this information to further deplete ocean resources. But it was already happening, and the oceans were being suffocated by pollution. All ocean species were affected by overfishing, runoff and other human threats. Even worse, the climate was changing. The oceans were warming, and the precious coral reefs were dying. The fate of the planet was at stake. Dolphins like native people, from what SeaWalker understood, never took more than they needed, ensuring that the fish populations would continue to be strong. Unfortunately, a few greedy people had upset the balance, which had created an environmental catastrophe. All of the animals in the sea were there for a reason. And now all were threatened. If one animal was hunted, such as sharks, it upsets the balance of the oceans and sets into motion a catastrophic environmental event that may never be reversed. The ocean needed a warrior, and SeaWalker felt that he could be a warrior for both worlds. There was no choice now. His destiny had arrived. And he was eager to begin. He knew instinctively that he must take action to change the way people treated the water planet. There needed to be a treaty for all life on land and in the sea. He was optimistic he could share his knowledge with people on the land and inspire them to care.

SeaWalker knew what he had to do, and time was running out. He had seen the devastation and depletion of the ocean realm and now wanted to take action to ensure the health of the planet and all its inhabitants. It was his time to take a stand for the rights of his fellow aquatic citizens.

The truth is, he had grown up stronger and faster than virtually all the dolphins in his tribe, even Cronos. Like Cronos, he had the strength and speed to overwhelm any predator in the ocean, except for maybe that mutation that he encountered in the deep, unforgiving sea. His confidence had grown, and he was no longer young SeaWalker but a force to be reckoned with. His gentle nature and goodwill are part of his character, but physically and mentally, he was an ocean warrior ready for battle!

*Ancient warriors of the land, and now*
*one of the sea...*

*W*

# CHAPTER FIFTEEN

# TOXIC SEA

**S**eaWalker's ocean paradise was turning into a toxic soup of industrial waste and a garbage dump for all of humanity. It was now affecting all life in the sea. The heart of the planet, the ocean, where all life began was threatened by one species: man. Unfortunately, humans had not made the connection that this was poisoning the very thing that provided them with a planet that was hospitable (at least up until the industrial age).

The ocean provides. It produces over 50% of the earth's oxygen and food for its ocean inhabitants as well as the eight billion walkers on land. No ocean... no life! What if SeaWalker and all the aquatic animals removed toxic waste and dumped it in the humans' backyard, how would they feel? Well, that was exactly what is happening to all the marine life. And it was getting worse each passing moon. The reality was that, whatever toxic waste ended up on land, finds its way to the sea through the water cycle. When it rains, it flushes all those chemicals into the rivers, lakes, streams, ponds and wetlands, and eventually, they find their way into the one ocean. SeaWalker realized that he must communicate from a two worlds' perspective, inspiring the human race to change how it deals with toxic waste and other pollutants. He wanted to make them see what they were doing. That day cannot come soon enough!

Humans had long thought that anything they dumped into the ocean was out of sight and out of mind. But the future of humanity is at risk. The water planet was now at a tipping point, and without direct action from all of its inhabitants, from all parts of the world, the health of the planet was in peril. At the rate that the humans were destroying the environment, it had become unsustainable. The problem for SeaWalker and all other inhabitants of the undersea world was that what happens on land affects all water habitats. What scientists and the intelligent sea animals knew instinctively was that water connected the entire Earth's biosphere, and all life depended on clean water and a healthy ocean.

Never had the threat been closer to home from both above and below the sea. The air, the land and the sea were being poisoned at an alarming rate. It was only a matter of time until the planet itself took revenge. When were the humans going to wake up and decide to be protectors instead of predators of the water planet? The true scale of man's impact on the planet was now being realized.

The horrifying toxic death of the sea and land was killing humans and animals at rates never seen in history. The tons of plastic entering the ocean taking hundreds of years to break down into micro plastics is being consumed by some of the smallest animals, like plankton and krill, that are then eaten by smaller fish which in turn are eaten by larger fish that are themselves eaten by dolphins and other marine animals and eventually then consumed by humans. It was breaking down all of their marine systems. From the bottom to the top of the food chain, man was poisoning the inhabitants of the entire planet.

Never before had SeaWalker and his family seen so much plastic in their ocean home. Sea turtles were consuming plastic bags which look like one of their main food staples, jellyfish. Once a plastic bag is ingested, the turtle eventually dies a slow, painful death. Even the seabirds were found with stomachs full of different types of plastic, such as bottle caps and other debris that they mistake for food. Humans were dumping tons of plastic into the oceans from nearly every place around the world. SeaWalker's dolphin family was at the top of the food chain. They ingested the plastic from the fish that they ate, and their calves were contaminated by their own mother's milk. It is estimated that nearly ten million tons of plastic end up in the ocean each year. This plastic was lethal, not only to the dolphins and SeaWalker, but virtually every animal in the ocean realm. The oceans that were once thought to be so vast that humans could do nothing to affect them were now so toxic that they may never recover. Dolphins and whales were the canaries in the coal mine…, and they are now dieing in mass numbers.

SeaWalker was also told by the elders that they had come upon some new islands that were not even islands at all. They were plastic islands. Some were even larger than the seven hundred islands in the Bahamas Archipelago. Could it be this toxic waste that was causing mass strandings of great whales around the globe? SeaWalker felt strongly that it had damaged the organs of many cetaceans. There were already so many threats. Now, through the poisoning of the oceans, which have provided for tens of millions of years, was destroying and pushing their species towards extinction.

*Poison the land and it will find its way*
*to the life-giving sea...*

*W*

# CHAPTER SIXTEEN

# EMPTY OCEANS

*M*arine pollution was coming from virtually every land base on the planet. There were also massive amounts of plastic and toxic waste being dumped from surface ships, both large and small. Much of the waste that was discarded found its way into the ocean and was picked up by the Gulf Stream. It was like a massive conveyor belt that moved the discarded waste from land into all parts of the ocean. Now, it was wreaking havoc on all marine life. Each year, thousands died from the toxic sea. It was time for a sea change.

SeaWalker decided that he wanted to investigate some of the other places in his Archipelago. He wanted to see the damage firsthand and had decided to become an ocean citizen scientist. He decided to head to a place called Bimini. The water had been described by his elders, as some of the most pristine and azure blue in the Universe. In fact, some even called it Bimini blue. He set off early on his quest to see the amazing living coral reefs and abundance of exotic fish life. From the smallest colorful reef fish to the larger schooling jacks, he was excited to visit the place that his family had told him about since
he was a small... whatever he was. The two-hour swim allowed

# CHAPTER SIXTEEN

him time to think deeply about things he was learning regarding the health of the oceans and the planet itself.

Amazingly, throughout the entire journey, he had not seen a single fish, large or small. No marine life whatsoever. He finally came upon a place that he was told had an abundance of living coral and vast amounts of fish and other aquatic animals. As he swam closer, he realized that everything was dead. As far as he could see, there was no life. A coral graveyard that stretched for miles and miles without one fish. This brought tears to SeaWalker's eyes. How could a pristine, beautiful place, a paradise in such a lush ocean be dead? How could this possibly happen?

The abundance of marine life that was described in detail was dead: From the giant coral that reached toward a cathedral of light, piercing the sheer surface and giving life to a wide variety of soft and hard corals. Brain corals as large as any structures that he had seen and other staghorn coral fields along with sponges that you could actually swim into. All of these corals were home to thousands of different marine species. Schools of fish of every size and color, and beautiful sea turtles. Even the eight-legged cephalopods, the octopus, who many of the marine animals considered the smartest in the ocean realm. Even the sharks had disappeared, not one to be found. It seemed like the entire ocean was affected by the death of the coral reefs. Between overfishing and pollution from the humans and the rising ocean temperature, it seemed the entire imminent Bimini biosphere was now extinct. Finally, SeaWalker couldn't take it anymore and sat on the sandy seafloor to contemplate how anyone could destroy such a beautiful undersea world. SeaWalker had seen beautiful, living reefs and now saw the polar opposite. He saw a coral graveyard that contained no life. And extinction that could continue to affect the health of not only the ocean but the entire water planet itself. His family told SeaWalker that even the sharks that were a threat to the sick animals played a critical role in the health of the ocean. Every single animal, large and small, and the animals that were part of the coral kingdom mattered. The sad thing was that it all came back to his species, the humans. They only had themselves to blame. Now there was a reckoning. The humans would now face extinction along with sea and other animals. Would they now decide to protect their environment, both on land and in the sea? SeaWalker, although deeply disturbed, decided that he would, from this moment on, do his part to enlighten humans to the dangers that they brought to themselves. In fact, he would enlighten all life of these perils. Not taking action was not an option for SeaWalker, and he rose to the surface to take a look at the beautiful sunset on the horizon. As he looked out across the sunlit waters, he realized that looking at just the surface, one could not see all the problems that were affecting the majority of the planet below.

# CHAPTER SIXTEEN

How could he now inspire the perpetrators of this global disaster?
He would find a way... and soon!

*Today, the sea is becoming empty*
*due to one species, man...*

*W*

# CHAPTER SEVENTEEN

# GRAVEYARD

SeaWalker decided that it was time to make his way toward land. Heading due west towards the east coast of the United States, he soon came upon a graveyard of ships, from large battleships to small sailing vessels, even a Navy submarine. The ships were scattered across the rocky bottom, some seemed to be hundreds of years old, and some looked very new. It was quite an underwater spectacle. Weren't these things supposed to be on top of the surface, and how did they get here? His natural curiosity led him to a German submarine where the top hatch door was open. Without hesitation, he swam through the vessel that was home to great schools of fish, a giant grouper and many large barracuda. The fish seemed right at home and in fact these sunken ships were artificial reefs that gave shelter to many of the coral reef inhabitants - from the smallest minnows to sea turtles to large sharks. SeaWalker swam through the many chambers, some still holding the skeletons of humans. Kind of scary, SeaWalker thought. Just then, a tiger shark swept through the main corridor, and SeaWalker quickly moved aside like a bullfighter, just barely surviving the shark attack. The shark turned one hundred and eighty degrees, and SeaWalker quickly disappeared into a torpedo chamber. The shark was ramming against the opening, attempting to eat this new dish. Fortunately, the other side of the torpedo chamber was open, and SeaWalker quickly swam through it to the other side of the submarine where he saw an old pirate ship. A closer look revealed cannons and twisted masts and the remnants of a skull and crossbones flag. The area had been a haven for these marauders, as they pillaged all of the Caribbean waters. They weren't really a threat to our kind, SeaWalker thought. These freebooters were after human pleasures: gold, rum and women – maybe after a lot of rum, a manatee… nah! The sharks enjoyed them immensely as they seemed to be sinking these sailing vessels throughout the Caribbean. Many sharks told tales of the pirates tasting like tuna – but then, they always said everything tasted like that. The stories must be true, SeaWalker thought, as he entered the ship whose hull was filled with gold and coins from around the world. These things were of no use to SeaWalker and were considered a bad omen. But he couldn't resist. He had to take one of the coins. As he left the wreck, he heard a voice, a ghostly voice.

"Be you fish, or be you man," the voice said. "Speak!"

"What the…," SeaWalker saw an apparition of an old pirate sea Captain hovering in the water, his sword at hand.

The Captain rose slowly through, then above the hull.

# GRAVEYARD

"Who are ye that dare steals the treasure of the Ramblin' Rose?" "Return it at once, or I will cut off your hands and maybe your head."

SeaWalker did as the Captain bid. He returned the coin, letting it float down, down to its resting place. As he left, this time he heard loud laughing from the other drunken pirates. But he could see none. This gave him the creeps so he swam quickly away from the ship. Now he approached an aircraft carrier that looked like a small island on the bottom of the sea. It still had dozens of airplanes on deck. And then right before his eyes, he saw dozens of ghostly pilots, running for the airplanes. Without opening the doors bordering the cockpits, they entered getting ready for flights that never would be. Overhead, the dim outlines of spectral enemy aircraft strafed the ship, sending what might have once been described as men running across the deck. And then as quickly as the apparitions appeared, they disappeared. And the sea was all of a sudden dead silent.

SeaWalker had a big lump in his throat. But he realized that is wasn't a lump. He had his mouth wide open, and the crab, running for cover, was was inside and nearly swallowed. A loud hacking sound ensued, and he was dislodged like a missile, flying out from the back of SeaWalker's throat. Simultaneously, they said, "What the heck are you doing here?" "Looking for you," the crab said. "Where have you been?" "I've been exploring," SeaWalker answered. "I've been checking out this graveyard of ships, and let me tell you it's weird."

They both decided they had enough adventure for one day, and it was time to head back. Suddenly, everywhere they looked, zombie-like sailors walked towards them, as a mob of ghosts. All of them had their mouths wide open and a look of fear in their eyes. All still had the injuries from their accidents. It was frightening. The only thing to do was swim straight up as the zombie sailors walked right through each other and towards their own vessels.

"Climb on crab," SeaWalker said.

"We're getting the heck out of here, now. Before we become one of them."

And they made their way back again to the Triangle where life was always a bit more normal.

The crab wanted to talk about it, but SeaWalker didn't have much to say. He was confused about all these zombie sailors. How they got there? And why they appeared then disappeared? The look on their faces told a lot, but it did not tell the whole story. SeaWalker had a sinking suspicion that he hadn't heard the last of the ghostly graveyard at this bottom of the sea.

*In the ocean, for the first time in the history of our planet, there were graveyards of dead coral and no life...*

*W*

# CHAPTER EIGHTEEN

# GHOST SHIP

**S**eaWalker's visit to the undersea graveyard kept him awake throughout the night and before the sun could even rise, he left his lava tube cave and headed straight back to the graveyard.

As he approached the ghost ships, he had an eerie feeling. The water was dark and mysterious, and the graveyard was drawing him near like a magnetic field. Many of the ships were positioned along the sea floor like buildings in a small city... make that a large city. Some of the massive ships even resembled skyscrapers that had tumbled over on their side, one a giant cruise ship from the 60's. In the center of the graveyard was a large Navy battleship that seemed to be the focus of the undersea graveyard. And as strange as this may sound, there was an iridescent, green glow that seemed to be illuminating from the inner body of the ship.

As SeaWalker approached the large battleship, he heard what sounded like dozens of people talking, whispering really. As he got closer, he realized that many sailors were talking amongst themselves and seemed to be waiting for his arrival. As SeaWalker got closer, the sailors became very quiet until the Captain of the vessel saluted him and welcomed him aboard.

# CHAPTER EIGHTEEN

"I am Captain Dwayne B. Sully of the U.S. Peacekeeper. Many of our men have disappeared over the years, but a lot of us are still here. I am not sure how long we have been here, but it seems like forever."

The Captain put out his hand, and as SeaWalker reached out to embrace it, he realized it was only a hologram. He didn't want to freak out the Captain so he went along with the handshake and tried to put on the best face possible considering the strange circumstance. Joining the Captain and SeaWalker on the bridge were at least three dozen sailors, all dressed in uniform, all standing at attention and hanging on the Captain's every word. SeaWalker told the Captain that he had been in the area yesterday and was hoping that the Captain could tell him about the graveyard of ships.

"I don't really remember how it all happened," the Captain began. "We were making our way across the Atlantic and, out of no where, the sea became angry and in a moment, she took us like an ocean tornado. We left the surface, violently crashing to the sea floor. Many of the men, including myself, became unconscious, and to be honest, I am still not sure if we have awakened. Every day we hope that our government will come for us. It is the only hope we have. We were hoping that you would have some information that might help us."

"I wish I did," SeaWalker said. "But I am still trying to figure everything out myself. I know there is some type of magnetic pull here, and this seems to be the center of it. I also know there are other beings present – many types of intelligence. Some seem to be from another Universe, not of land or sea, but somewhere up there beyond the planets and stars."

The Captain eagerly agreed, "So you've seen them, too?" "Only from a distance," says SeaWalker. "What do they want?" asked the Captain. "What could they want from us?"

SeaWalker assured the Captain that he would do his best to find out and would not let him down. The Captain said that he had to take care of his ship and his crew and he hoped to see SeaWalker again soon. And at that moment, the Captain and crew completely disappeared.

Somehow, SeaWalker was not fazed after all he had seen and decided to continue his journey. The city seemed to be both alive and dead at the same time. There was a presence, a life force; you could feel it in the water. Now the sunlight began to pierce the surface, illuminating the strange world below. There were not only ships of every size and shape - hundreds of them - there were also airplanes of every imaginary type – jumbo jets to fighter planes from World War I. There were even a couple of

# CHAPTER EIGHTEEN

surfboards, old cars and trucks.

SeaWalker thought, Weren't those supposed to be floating on the surface? Something was definitely strange in this place. Suddenly, SeaWalker felt something behind him. He turned around and was staring into the eyes of a beautiful sea-maiden. His fellow tribesman told stories of these sirens of the sea. Her hair was red like fire and her eyes green. Then he noticed something strange. She had a tail not unlike the fish scales on some of the animals he had caught and consumed. She was floating weightless like him, and her eyes pierced his. Without saying a word, SeaWalker felt a sensation. She seemed to be putting a spell on him. He was mesmerized by her beauty and smile. He waited for her to say something, but she never did. Was she telepathic like him? He couldn't wait and decided to introduce himself,

"I am SeaWalker. I live with the dolphin tribe at the edge of the Triangle."

At this she smiled even wider and moved in closer. Her long arms reached out and embraced him. Slowly, she moved her face up close to his and their noses touched. SeaWalker was having all these strange feelings for the first time. The sea-maiden looked deep into his eyes, into his soul really. No words were spoken, but the chemistry was mutual. Finally, their two bodies came together. And then suddenly, she broke apart and swam towards the east without saying a word, but continued to look at him over her shoulder. SeaWalker was stunned, but he decided to follow her anyway.

What could this mean? Who was this siren of the sea? He had to find out.

She swam down through a deep cavern, deeper and deeper into a magical undersea garden covered with beautiful coral reefs and many colorful schools of fish. She only paused for a moment to look over her shoulder again and smile at SeaWalker. A short time later, she seemed to arrive at her destination, a coral den where SeaWalker could easily see more than two-dozen mermaids, including some younger ones. He was greeted warmly, and a number of the mermaids embraced him from all sides, all with warm smiles. Ironically, none of them spoke, only communicating with their eyes and facial expressions. This was fine for SeaWalker as he was too stunned to say anything. He was captivated by their beauty. For the first time, he was feeling shy and nervous. He decided to wave goodbye and continue his tour of the graveyard of ships.

All of the sea-maidens lined up to wave him goodbye and give him a warm smile. The first one even blew him a kiss.

# CHAPTER EIGHTEEN

SeaWalker made his way back to the ships and came upon a rusty old fishing boat. As he swam around to the back, he noticed an old, bearded man with two sons. They warmly greeted him and invited him to join them at the back of the vessel. These men had a ghostly presence but were real enough.

The Captain yelled out, "Ey, lad! Where you be from?"

SeaWalker told him, and the Sea Captain smiled and said, "Be careful, there's beings out here that will take you and steal your soul. My youngest boy was taken. They put him in a trance and, in a tunnel of light, he rose to the surface and entered some type of alien spaceship. We tried to stop him, but we couldn't. A few weeks later, we saw him, and he seemed to be in an altered state. He was not the same; he was changed, not in the present reality. A short time later, he disappeared again, and we have not seen him since. I only have two sons left. If they take anybody, I hope they take me. I am old and probably don't have much time. I hope they take me."

"I saw these aliens," SeaWalker said. "I am not sure why they are taking people, but they seem to need them to survive. Maybe I can try and figure out why they are doing this. I am not sure if they speak the same language or how they communicate. I am actually scared to talk to them, but I will try to find out what happened to your son. As soon as I figure this all out, I will come back."

The Captain seemed to get a tear in his eye. SeaWalker's eyes were also moist, and he could feel for the father who lost his son. It was the first time that he wondered about his own father. Who was his father, and would he ever meet him? Had he been taken by the aliens?

*Ghost ship full of lost souls now resting
on the bottom of the sea - not dead or alive
but something in between...*

*W*

# CHAPTER NINETEEN

# OCEAN ALLIANCE

Just before making his way back, SeaWalker noticed a massive blue tunnel of light piercing the surface, illuminating what appeared to be a small city at the sea floor. Curious, he decided to swim over for a look. As he got closer, he couldn't believe he was actually looking at an alien space camp, a futuristic city of polished stainless steel. There was almost a toxic glow around the entire biosphere. There was also a strange vibration that got stronger as he moved closer to the alien city, like a force field. Part of the city looked like a futuristic factory, and SeaWalker eagerly swam over to a large porthole to have a look. Indeed, it was an exceptionally large assembly line factory with giant machines prodding and probing hundreds of humans in a trance like state, as they moved across a conveyor belt.

Towards the end of the belt, a stainless steel cap dropped on top of each of the humans' heads with a large flash of light and an electrical voltage eminating from the cap. When the cap was removed, the humans were empty shells and in a lifeless zombie- like state. And finally, at the end of the line, they were dropped into a large dumpster. The whole thing made SeaWalker squeamish, but he couldn't take his eyes off of this factory. It was

# CHAPTER NINTEEN

surreal. It seemed to be fully automated with machines running the entire facility except for a few weird alien creatures milling around. The aliens seemed to come in three different sizes; some very small and dwarf-like, some quite tall, and then there were the giants – all with egg-shaped oversized heads with giant, black bug-eyes and two small holes for their nostrils. The mouths seemed to only be a hole in the middle of the chin. Their slim long arms had large hands and long fingers with skinny suction cups. Their bodies were thin and fit, and their legs were skinny with large feet and three toes. Their skin was ghostly white except for their mouth area, which was dark purple. The smaller ones seemed to be the worker bees. The medium sized aliens seemed to be the bosses, with the larger ones being the enforcers.

When the dumpster was full, it was pushed over to a human recycling room. The door was closed and green gas was pumped into the glass room. Slowly, the humans came back to life. But was it really life? What kind of life could this be, living in purgatory - slaves to the aliens who possessed their minds, bodies and souls? The aliens seemed to be removing the life force for their own benefit. SeaWalker decided to swim over to the other end of the building. Spaceships were lined up like buses, and people were being marched into the factory. They seemed to be under some type of spell. When one spaceship was unloaded, the next pulled up and unloaded even more. There must have been at least two hundred spaceships and buses lined up. After the spaceship unloaded, it rose through a beam of light piercing the surface, and then it was gone, followed by the next and the next and the next...

Then, all of a sudden, SeaWalker was surrounded! The aliens did not speak, but somehow SeaWalker knew they wanted him to go with them. He resisted at first. He then decided that this was a bad idea so he decided to go and see what all this was about. A door opened into the factory, and SeaWalker was escorted down the hallway to a large room and then into a holding area. And then the door closed. Alone in the room, he began to wonder, Are these aliens going to zap me of my life and energy? Should I get the heck out of here? Try to escape? In the end, he decided to try and communicate with them.

The door opened, and two aliens floated towards him. They did not speak but telepathically communicated that they meant him no harm and to come with them to meet their superior. After a short elevator ride to the top of the factory, SeaWalker was escorted to a large, sterile room. Greeting him was the chief alien who they called Higa. He put his hand out with his fingers up and greeted SeaWalker. Without thinking, SeaWalker gave him a high-five and the chief was very surprised and nervously jumped back.

"Welcome to our camp, SeaWalker. I can see you are not human; you are not marine animal, but something different. I hope you didn't see anything disturbing. The humans we consume are really dead, but they don't know it. They are in between life and death. The service we provide helps them in their transition. We are here for them, and they are here for us. It is a symbiotic relationship really. You understand, don't you?"

"I really don't know what is going on," SeaWalker said. "All I know is that some of the people are scared."

"I assure you," Higa said, "there is no pain. It's really just food, kind of like when people are eating cows or dolphins or eating fish. We have been farming humans for thousands of years. I must tell you that their quality has diminished. They are full of toxic chemicals, and many of them taste funny. We are actually doing them a huge favor like the sharks in the ocean that eat the weak and keep the oceans healthy. Their populations would grow out of control without us. We need each other."

"Have you discussed this with their leaders?" SeaWalker asked.

"Their leaders are really part of our family now," says Higa. "We have, through technology, been able to replicate humans for hundreds of years. In fact, one of their presidents is really a man named Borgar from the planet Kremtis. If you really look at him, you can see that he is not a true human. We did make him an idiot, modeled after the last president, of course, so he would blend in. The average IQ of a human is about equal to the intelligence of our toenails – and that's the smart ones."

"This is way too much information for me," SeaWalker states. "But thank you anyway. I have to go now."

"You are free to leave, and I look forward to seeing you again. Please understand that what happens in this underwater galaxy, stays in this galaxy."

SeaWalker did an about face, and two guards took him to the outside of the factory where he made a beeline to the Triangle, thinking the entire way, "Oh my God! Oh my God! What did I just witness? Are any of us safe?"

*Humans have always been willing to support
the possibility of intelligence on other planets
before they consider ours...*

*W*

# CHAPTER TWENTY

# ABDUCTION

S eaWalker was awoken by a strange dream. He had been abducted during the night, mysterious and unimaginable even after all he's been through. "Walker, we are your parents. I am your father, and this is your mother. You haven't seen us for a very long time, since the storm. You were a small baby, but we have always been here for you. We have been here looking over you your whole life, and now we are all reunited."

SeaWalker stood up straight in bed rubbing his eyes in disbelief. Could these really be his parents? He didn't really remember them, but they seemed to be and this, if true, was a fantastic moment. The parents continued to smile widely and reached out for Walker. "Please come with us now, young Walker. You have grown to be such a strong young man. Please come with us now so that we may tell you of our long journey.

SeaWalker jumped out of his bed and embraced his father and mother together.

Is this real? Is this really happening? he thinks. It is! It is! It's a joyous moment for all of them.

The parents held SeaWalker's hand as they enticed him to leave his home and head out to sea with them once again. They seemed real, so real, but something didn't seem right. SeaWalker was overcome by the thought that he had found his long, lost parents. Side by side, they sat together near the sea floor. The parents asked him how he was and what had he been doing and who were his friends? SeaWalker told them about the tribe and how the dolphins came to be his family. He started sharing some of the early times and stories of his life. The parents were fascinated and reassuring. They assured him that now they were back together and everything would be fine.

SeaWalker was so taken by being reunited with his family that he didn't even consider where they were. He didn't care. He was just so happy. He was in the moment when he realized after a couple of hours they were back at the space camp near the factory where he had been the day before witnessing the humans being processed by the aliens.

"Why are we here?" SeaWalker said to his parents.

"Well, this place is OK. These are my friends," the father assured SeaWalker. "They are with us, and they are our host. They have provided shelter to your mom and I over the years, and they will also take care of you now."

Next to the processing factory was a large spaceship that seemed to be a sphere made out of a type of metal with a stainless steel finish. As they approached, a wide door opened and a ramp slid down towards their feet. The parents held SeaWalker by the arms, and together, they entered the spaceship. SeaWalker was still focused on the fact that he was with his parents and was oblivious to everything happening around him. As soon as they entered the giant spaceship, in the main corridor, the entry floor slid back into the ship and the doors closed silently behind them. The spaceship was dimly lit, and there were many small aliens working at computers at different stations. An alien spoke first, "Ah, SeaWalker, I am so glad you have reunited with your parents and you could come and visit us here. We have been waiting for you for a long time, and now you are here. Now you are back home with your parents."

SeaWalker was still very excited by the presence of his parents, and now they were all welcomed to the ship.. Everything he had done in the past seemed small compared to this reunion. He had thought about this moment for his entire life.

SeaWalker followed his parents and the alien to a dining room area where they sat at a large table. A number of small alien waiters brought out silver covered platters where they were presented with a wide variety of very strange looking food, very strange indeed. There were even paintings up on the wall by an artist named Wyland that featured many of the marine animals SeaWalker knew. The waiters served guests without hesitation. He followed his parents and the alien, and they began to eat some of the strange creatures, some of them moving around on the plate in front of them. The parents looked very normal eating the dishes, and SeaWalker followed after watching them use the utensils. The alien also used the utensils and just shoveled the food into the little hole in his chin. It was a little odd, but then again, SeaWalker had seen some very strange creatures in the ocean so he was not overly creeped out. The food had very little taste, and the texture was strange, kind of slimy and slippery and very gooey. It seemed like before he could even chew the food, it simply slid down his throat and into his stomach. The parents seemed anxious to make an impression on young SeaWalker and continuously smiled widely at him and embraced him with their eyes. SeaWalker smiled too and looked lovingly at his mother and father. He hadn't seen them since the big storm in the Bermuda Triangle when he was a baby, and even now, he didn't remember it. He was told by the other members of the dolphin tribe about this event and assumed that his parents went down with the boat. He recalled they were sailing, and he was rescued and brought to a volcanic vent where the gases from the ancient sea gave him life and saved him from the perils of drowning in the deep abyss. Other than that, he had no memory of his parents, but they were quick to tell him about their lives and how important he was to them and how they could now be together forever.

"We have been searching for you for years and years and years, and our friends here have helped us finally find you. When you came yesterday, they contacted us and said, 'We believe we have found your son.' And here you are with us at this moment. We are truly blessed and want to do everything we can to be with you, to share this world and other worlds with you. You are our son, Walker, and we are together at last."

The alien joined in, "Yes, Walker, this is a moment that all of us have been waiting for. You are a member of our family now, and everything we have will be shared with you – all the knowledge of the Universe and beyond. Everything we have is yours. You are one of us. Our tribe is billions of years old. We came from a planet very much like this one but in a larger galaxy far, far away from this one. Our civilization was very advanced, not like this primitive one, not like the ones above that seek to destroy the very planet that gives them life. We have watched in horror for the last hundred years as this planet has been torn apart, wars among people and worse yet, a war on the planet itself. They have poisoned the air, land and sea. They have slaughtered nearly every species of ocean animals, and this century looks like it could be the last for this selfish species so we are here to do what we can. Years ago they dropped a nuclear bomb that gave us a wakeup call, but to be honest with you, I don't think we can save them. You are one of us, so we plan to save you and your parents and take you with us when this planet is destroyed completely."

Finally, it sank in. SeaWalker said without hesitation, "What about my family? What about my tribe? The dolphins, the whales, my friend the crab, the lost souls that I have just met... what will become of them?"

"I am not sure I understand," said the alien.

SeaWalker, now with more passion said very directly, "The family that I have, what will happen to them? What will become of them now?"

"Unfortunately SeaWalker, they may go the way of the larger animals, the dinosaurs. They will be extinct as will the human race. It is only a matter of time before the planet takes them. We are only using what we need to ensure our species survives this planet's ultimate destruction in this century."

# ABVUCTION

That was almost too much for young SeaWalker to take. He realized that the fate of his family, friends and the poor humans that he has met, most who were not dead or alive but kind of in the middle, were all doomed. SeaWalker was now in a panic. "Can we not save them? Can we not save the blue planet? Can we not turn the tide? What can we do to heal our planet and save the tribe and my friends and these poor, lost souls? We need to do something for them. Please!"

Now the parents chime in, "Walker, you must understand that the humans have been on a course of destruction for nearly one hundred years. They have taken from the earth, and now, the oceans are warming, the land is poisoned and the fish are nearly gone. The oceans are empty. There will not be enough food for anyone to survive. There will be no clean water to drink. The aliens are actually doing the human race and our friends in the sea a favor. That's why we have joined with them. We want you with us when we decide to leave this dying planet. Pretty soon, we must leave."

SeaWalker was now torn. The reality of losing his new family and friends in the sea was almost too much for him to bear. He began to get teary-eyed and held his head in his hands. He was trying not to cry, but on the inside, he was shaken. His parents put their hands on his back and tried to reassure him, but he sprang

# CHAPTER TWENTY

up and said, "NO! I can't allow this to happen. I made promises that I would't allow this to happen. This can't be happening."

The alien was upset now, "It's too late! It is already happening. It has been happening for a long time. We are at the end of time for this planet. You must join us if you and your family are going to survive."

It was at this point that SeaWalker could no longer stand what he was hearing. He stood up abruptly and said, "I have to go now, please. I have to go be with my tribe. Please understand."

His parents tried to stop him, but the alien said, "Please let him go." SeaWalker made his way towards the exit of the spaceship. The door opened, and he sadly swam out, back towards his tribe. His mind was racing. Was this apparition really his parents? How could he know? The fact was that he really never saw his parents. He was only six months old when he was rescued by his tribe. Was this all a lie to take him away... to get him on their side? The unexplainable phenomenon he had witnessed gave him pause. It felt like he was in the Twilight Zone. He needed to get far away so he could think clearly.

*In ancient Greece, the killing of a dolphin*
*was equal to killing a man...*

*W*

# CHAPTER TWENTY-ONE

# LAND CALLING

Upon his arrival in the Triangle, for the first time in a long time, SeaWalker slept in. He slept and slept and slept. He slept for over twenty hours. When he finally did get up, he couldn't believe that he had finally met his parents, finally met the two people he had thought about from the very beginning. But the idea that his parents were somehow connected to the aliens made him wonder. Why would they be together and why were they strongly directing him to join them without concern for his tribe, his new family? His curious nature told him that he needed to go to the land to see the walkers in order to get a different perspective. Maybe even try to find his birthplace. Even though he knew they may be evil and dangerous, he had to see for himself.

He had never been on land before – at least since the very beginning of his life that he remembered, but he had an instinct that land was to the east and had heard stories from migrating whales that there was land and it was far, far to the east. So, he headed away for the sunset and began his long journey to finally visit the other world of land.

SeaWalker swam and swam and swam, but he did not tire. His

desire to finally go see land and experience things for himself was driving him. He swam until the sun set and all through the night, until the sun started to rise behind him. After mid-day, he finally saw the shape of a landmass – a large island. He swam even faster towards this large, dark shape on the horizon. It was late afternoon now, and SeaWalker began to realize that this was not an island at all but a huge mass rising from the sea. From north to south, the landmass covered the horizon completely. With the warm sun in his eyes now, he made his way inland to a beach area where the water and land came together. Suddenly, he began to hear a lot of noise, a lot more noise than he had ever heard. He raised his head above the surface to see dozens of boats on top of the water... in every direction – small, fast boats and large ocean liners. There were boats everywhere and it was very chaotic. The only boats he had ever seen before laid still on the ocean floor, and now, the boats were racing all around him.

All of a sudden, the noise became intense. Just as he raised his head above water, a very fast, small boat nearly ran over the top of him as he duck-dived at the last second to avoid the sharp propellers. As the boat passed, he realized that these humans were dangerous in these quick, little vessels and that he had to be very aware.

But there it was, right in front of him now – land. Finally land.

# LAND CALLING

What would it be like? Soon he would find out. Soon he would set his first foot on land. He was almost there. Right in front of him, only a few yards away, was the beach. The sun was beginning to set now, and he was swimming in very shallow water, only three feet deep. Now two feet. One foot. He literally had to crawl on his hands and knees up onto the beach. Thankfully, there were no people on this part of the beach. He crawled up on the white-yellow sand and rose to his feet. A funny thing happened as he made his way up onto the beach. As he began to dry from the sun, he began to change. His flippers became feet, and his dorsal fin retracted. His webbed fingers became, well, just normal fingers. He was becoming human. After a couple of minutes, he was completely dry and fully human, but it was a very uncomfortable for him to stand up. It was almost like being on a ship at sea for months and trying to get your land legs. He was like a drunken sailor stumbling around on the beach trying to get his sea legs – or in this case, his human legs. The shore was very exciting for SeaWalker, and the fact that he was standing upright and walking on the above world was a great thrill. He noticed that the beach led up to an area covered in green stuff. He made his way up through the greenery – grass, trees and the plants – and it was unlike anything he had seen in the ocean. At that moment, he turned around and caught the last glimpse of the sun as it descended in front of the horizon.

As SeaWalker began walking on the land, he was approached by a black, fuzzy looking hairy animal. He froze for a moment but then realized that the animal was friendly, wagging its tail and telepathically reaching out to him. The animal sensed that he was different than the animals that lived on land permanently. They both kind of sized each other up. The dog ran a few circles around SeaWalker, and he chased the dog around as well. When they finally came together, SeaWalker knelt down, and the dog came over. SeaWalker embraced the dog, and they had a great encounter.

After a moment, the dog licked SeaWalker's face and took off in another direction. SeaWalker decided to follow the animal and began to walk very swiftly in the direction of the dog who was running in an open field of grass. Eventually, he was running too with his new legs! He was very uncoordinated, falling down and getting back up to his feet, laughing hysterically. He seemed to be enjoying this new body that was made not for the sea but for land. Right in front of him was a small boat harbor with very still water and large wooden docks. He noticed a small group of men sitting around a table having a little meeting of the minds almost like his dolphin tribe. He felt uncomfortable about being discovered so he found a large bush to hide behind and listen in. The men seemed to be having a great time. They were smoking cigars and seemed to be drinking out of bottles that SeaWalker had seen on the ocean floor. He could hear them excitedly talking about fishing, catching fish and how one guy caught the biggest fish. They all laughed, and it appeared like they were all fisherman. They were very excited at the catch. In fact, SeaWalker noticed in horror as over a dozen large fish that looked like tuna were strung up along a line near the boat. The fish were bleeding and hung upside down. Their weight had distorted their streamline shape, hanging from large metal hooks. It was very grotesque and sad. The last thing SeaWalker wanted to do was be hung upside down like one of the fish on the rope, so he was very careful. But he couldn't stop himself from listening to their conversation. He noticed also, as it got dark outside, some lights illuminating the table where the fishermen were sitting and also on the docks going out to the boats. It was kind of like the light from a full moon illuminating SeaWalker's home in the sea. All of a sudden, SeaWalker came in for a closer look and tripped on a rock. He came out into the open. All the men turned and stared and one of them came right over to SeaWalker and said, "Are you okay, son?"

"Yeah, yeah. I am okay," replied SeaWalker. The older man helped SeaWalker to his feet and put his arm around him. SeaWalker noticed a strange smell coming from the man who was acting kind of goofy. But he was very nice. The old man asked SeaWalker to join the group. But SeaWalker said, "No, no.

# CHAPTER TWENTY-ONE

That's okay. I am actually just traveling through."


The old man said, "No, you come over here with us son and sit down and have a beer." SeaWalker didn't know what a beer was, but he thought he would go over and join the group for a while. The group of large older, men all slid over a little bit, and SeaWalker sat down. They were consuming many of these bottles. In fact, there were dozens of empty ones scattered all over the ground. They popped one open and handed it to SeaWalker saying, "Here you go, kid." SeaWalker wasn't quite sure what to make of it, but he watched the others kind of toast it up and drink it down so that he would follow their example. SeaWalker didn't really notice that at some point they stopped drinking so he just kept drinking and drinking and drinking until eventually he had drank the whole bottle. He let out a very large burp, which made the men laugh hysterically.


Ironically, the five men were so drunk that none of them noticed that SeaWalker didn't have any clothes on, and apparently, SeaWalker didn't know either. But when one of the men got up to go to the restroom and looked down and saw SeaWalker's bare behind, he kind of giggled and said, "Son, what happened to your bathing suit?"


SeaWalker looked at him kind of curious and said, "What's a

bathing suit?"

The old man just started laughing and slapped him on the back. SeaWalker looked around. All of the men were wearing shorts. So, at this point, he figured it was too late and decided to just let the table cover him up and have a couple more beers with the guys. The guys really liked SeaWalker. He didn't say much, but he had a great smile. That was good because the guys did a lot of the talking – and the more they drank, the louder they got and the more stories they told. A lot of the stories really didn't mean a whole lot to SeaWalker, but he was entertained none-the-less.

After a couple of hours, SeaWalker excused himself. The guys thought that he had to use the restroom, but SeaWalker actually thought it was time to go. He had seen enough and it was time to continue his investigation of the land.

On the way out, he noticed an old pair of torn up shorts and decided that they would be important if he was going to blend in. Since that they didn't seem to belong to anyone, he quickly put them on. They were much larger than he needed, so he took a little rope and tied them off, and he was good to go. He decided that it was getting late and maybe he should try to rest. So he found a grassy area very near the beach where he decided to curl up into a ball and get some sleep.

# CHAPTER TWENTY-ONE

SeaWalker was suddenly awoken by some human voices close to where he was sleeping. He looked over the hedge and saw a couple humans, younger, two with very long hair. One seemed to be female. As he looked over the hedge, he was noticed by the two and the male yelled, "Hey Bro! What's up?"

SeaWalker said, "Hey!"

The guy said, "Hey, you want to smoke some weed?" SeaWalker said, "Smoke what?"

"I got some nice herb."

"Well I don't really smoke."

"That's cool, Bro. You from around here?" "No, not really. No, I am from out there." "Oh, you live on the island."

"Yeah, kind of like that," SeaWalker said.

The girl chimed in, "You are very cool looking."

"What's cool?"

"You know, you're far out, man," she responded.

It seemed that SeaWalker found himself camping near two sort of hippies that were traveling and, at this point, homeless.

But, they were very positive and "go with the flow". SeaWalker sensed that they were not a threat and were supportive of him. Being homeless, they all had something in common. SeaWalker was invited to sit by the fire in the morning as they brewed some nice herb tea. They were also smoking some unusual cigarettes. SeaWalker couldn't help but notice the smell. It seemed the more they smoked, the more their eyes glazed over and closed. After a while, they were very hungry so the guy reached into his pocket. Earlier, he had scrounged through a nearby dumpster to get some leftover food. It didn't look very appetizing, but they were happy to share with SeaWalker, but he said, "That's okay. I am fine. I will get some fish later."

They said, "Aw. Are you a vegetarian?" He replied, "I don't know what that is?" "Well, do you eat meat and chicken?" "Primarily I just like fish."
"Well that's great, man. Awesome!"

The two asked SeaWalker how old he was. He really didn't know. They were guessing that he was in his late teens. SeaWalker thought that was about right. He asked, "How about you folks?"

They said, "We're eighteen."

They seemed to be about the same age. The couple was very affectionate and warm to SeaWalker. He could see in their eyes they were very friendly and didn't seem to be a threat at all. In fact, all the things he had heard about the "walkers", the humans, didn't ring true. They seemed harmless, friendly, and very easy going. He wondered, were all walkers like this? Just then, the female stood up and said, "let's go skinny dipping". She peeled off her shorts and top and ran out to the beach and dove into the ocean, followed closely by her long-haired, male friend. SeaWalker saw this as an opportunity to remove his shorts and make his way out to his ocean home. And as they all dove into the ocean, he began to change again. In a matter of minutes, his dorsal fin began to grow and his feet and fingers began to web again. The slits under his ears began to appear. But it was dark, and the hippies were so stoned that they really didn't notice any of it. SeaWalker decided that he had a good experience but maybe it was just time to get himself back to his tribe, back home. He looked at the couple, smiled warmly and said, "I hope to see you again," and began swimming out towards the horizon on his way back to the Triangle.

*Dolphins left the land tens of millions of years ago*
*in search of food never to return...*

*W*

# CHAPTER TWENTY-TWO

# ABOVE WORLD

Another perfect day in the Bermuda Triangle, SeaWalker decided to head out to this little island that he had spotted several months earlier. His confidence about the walkers had risen since his last encounter with the fishing dudes and hippies. So, he decided to go out on a little exploration, as he was naturally curious about everything. He approached the island. It was not a large island at all compared to the land that he visited when he met the drinking sailors. This one was quite small and not much above sea level, but it had lots of palm trees and coconuts and was very pretty. His curiosity peaked as he again entered the shallow water and then stepped onto a very light, sandy beach.

Within a couple minutes, he transformed again, into his human self. Again, he had problems with his land legs. He was kind of stumbling around, and his equilibrium was kind of messed up from spending almost all of his time underwater or floating on the sea. But now, he was SeaWalker and trying to get his land legs again. He was amazed by the beautiful land with its lush green trees and the many different colored flowers that reminded him of the coral reef he had seen below. The land was indeed a paradise and he felt like he had found it. He wanted to explore the island. He continued to walk through the lush gardens. He heard rushing water and realized there was a rainforest with a nice waterfall with little pools to swim in. This was, obviously for him, the best of both worlds. He, of course, was a creature of the water and of the land, so the island for him was truly a natural place, and he enjoyed it immensely. As he continued to hike around the island and through intense forest, he came upon a little area where there seemed to be a habitat, a little hut, kind of a grass roof hut along a little bay where there was very small boat. As he started walking towards this little house, he started to hear voices, not unlike some of the voices he had heard when he met the sailors and the hippies. He was cautious at first and decided to kind of stay back and watch. At one point, he saw a girl – a beautiful, young girl. Younger than the hippie girl he had seen before. She had long, flowing hair and was running towards the little lagoon, diving head long into it and rising slowly, running her hands through her long blonde hair. She seemed to smile very wide.

SeaWalker was mesmerized by her beauty. She seemed to radiate beauty and excitement in her island home. SeaWalker decided to get closer and stumbled on one of the tree trunks, falling down the beach path. He startled the girl. SeaWalker was a little embarrassed when the girl looked over and saw him; but she smiled deeply at this young man, somehow sensing that he was not a threat. SeaWalker, too embarrassed to say anything, just smiled back as she approached him, looking intensely at him trying to figure out where he came from. Finally, she said, "Hi, I'm Marina!"

SeaWalker continued to smile finally and said, "Hi, I'm SeaWalker!"

She started laughing hysterically. "SeaWalker? That's an unusual name."

"Well, my name was actually Walker, but my family calls me SeaWalker."

"Well, its great to meet you, and I am glad you are visiting our island."

"Oh, this is your island?"

"Well, my family doesn't really own it, but my dad knew the native family that has the rights, and they have allowed us to come here and spend a few months each year."

"Well that's great. This is the first time I've visited your island," said SeaWalker.

# CHAPTER TWENTY-TWO

"Would you like me to show you around?" said Marina.

"That sounds great!"

"Well, let's go. I'll take you around to see some of my favorite places. Its not very big, but it is very beautiful."

She grabbed his arm and began to walk him along the beach, very excited to have someone to share this island paradise. Somehow, she sensed SeaWalker was a good person, and she was eager to have a new friend. Sometimes, the island could become very lonely. Of course, Marina never had a problem enjoying her own time, but now she had a new friend to share things with. She couldn't be more excited! It was around noon with barely a cloud in the sky when Marina wanted to try to get some coconuts so that SeaWalker could have something to drink. She went to her favorite tree that was very low hanging. She climbed along a branch hacking off two coconuts using a machete that was left nearby. SeaWalker was amazed at how quickly she knocked off the outer skin and cut off the top of the coconut! She handed one to him so he could drink this sweet nectar of the islands. It tasted wonderful, especially on a hot day. After tasting sea water for so long it was perfect. They shared the coconut juice and afterwards, she cut the meat into small pieces. They continued their walk along the beach and then went into the tropical forest.

After a short time, they decided they would sit down in a small grassy area. They gazed into each other's eyes. It seemed to be love at first sight. Marina was only sixteen, and SeaWalker was probably seventeen. He didn't really even know his own age but he seemed to be about 17. So, for both of them, it was really a mutual crush. The eyes were all telling and Marina's eyes, big and brown, gazed into SeaWalker's aqua blue, clear eyes. She had no idea who he was or where he was from, but she knew there was something special about her new friend.

SeaWalker, of course, was very curious about this young girl but before he could say anything, she began to rattle off many questions... "Where did you come from? Where is your family? Have you been here before?" A multitude of questions. SeaWalker just simply smiled. Finally, he opened up, "I'm not sure where I was originally born, where I am from, but my family is out there – a place called the Triangle."

"The Bermuda Triangle?"

"Yes," SeaWalker said. "I've heard of that, she replied"

"Well, the Bermuda Triangle actually," Marina explained, "is a whole area out here. This island is part of it as well. It encompasses from south Florida to Bermuda to the Caribbean, and it has a long history of strange occurrences. A lot of people are very scared of the Triangle, but my family loves it here. We have been coming here since I was born, and this island in particular has fresh water and a place for us to grow vegetables and fruit. We come here each year for a couple of months with my parents. They are both professors and take  sabbaticals for the summer. I was born in Georgia but my family moved to south Florida, Ft. Lauderdale, where I grew up. Next year, I will graduate from high school."

"What's high school?" SeaWalker asked, looking at her very curiously.

She thought he was kidding and started laughing very loud. Her laugh was very contagious, and when she really got to laughing she snorted a little bit, which really made SeaWalker laugh. In fact, he himself snorted, and they both had a good, long laugh after that. It was an immediate friendship – one that SeaWalker hoped would continue for a long, long time.

She wanted to take SeaWalker to meet her parents, but he said he had to be back to be with his family and could not stay to long. She insisted that he stay a little longer and they continued to stare into each other's eyes and talk. SeaWalker was very curious about this young girl. How was her life? What did she enjoy? Where did she see herself in the future? Pretty deep questions from a guy she had just met, but she was very comfortable telling him a little bit about what she was thinking. She loved animals, and she wanted to be a vet. She had several animals including a little dog, a little Jack Russell. His name was Binky. She also had a turtle that she had adopted. It was a sea turtle that was injured when it was caught in a fishing net and lost a front flipper. She called it Junior. The little turtle was her favorite. Every once in a while she would take the turtle out to sea to play with it, and it always seemed to want to return with Marina. She would bring it back to her hut where she would rehab and feed it. She had a sense that the turtle understood she was a friend, and they had a very beautiful relationship. This made SeaWalker appreciate her even more as he too become friends with the turtles of the sea. He was not sure how Marina would react knowing that he was also a creature of the sea... and land. He didn't know if he would ever be able to tell her his true story, about growing up in the ocean and living with the animals of the sea and being able to communicate with them. Maybe one day he could share this deep secret, but for now, he was happy that they were talking and sharing some stories about their lives.

Time seemed to stand still as they looked into each other's eyes and told stories about their lives, but it was now approaching sunset. It was unbelievable that they had been talking non-stop for six hours. Both of them knew that somehow they fit together. They had come together for this moment, but soon, they hoped to be together to continue their stories and possibly their life's journey. Even though they had only known each other for one day, it felt like a lifetime for each of them. Finally, SeaWalker looking out at the sunset told Marina that he had to return home to his tribe. She understood, but she wanted to know when he would return.

"I am not sure when I can return, but I will come back as soon as I can. I promise."

She trusted him, and she gave him a big, long hug. It was almost as if she did not want to let go of him or let him leave. Eventually though, she let go and he turned around and headed back toward the sea. Just before he entered the water, he looked over his shoulder at her and smiled deeply - as did she. They could not take their eyes off each other, but finally, it was time to go. SeaWalker ran towards the water and took a big leap in and headed out towards his home in the Triangle, trying not to look back.

All the way back, he could not stop thinking about this girl who had somehow stirred his emotions. He had never felt this way before. His affections for her were running through his entire body. Everything in his DNA was inspired by the girl on the beach, and he thought only of her as he made the long journey back home.

*SeaWalker was born in a world so entirely different from his new family in the sea, now a new species, he had adapted to both..*

*W*

175

# CHAPTER TWENTY-THREE

# GIRL ON THE BEACH

SeaWalker tossed and turned all night dreaming about the beautiful girl he met on the beach. He could not stop thinking about her. In fact, the next day, he got up and told his friends, "I met this girl, this wonderful, beautiful girl." As he told his friends about his affection for her, his friend the crab kind of rolled his eyes like... Oh my God, what has happened to him? He was a whole new person, giddy and would not stop talking about her and his affection for her and how he could not stop thinking about her. Without hesitation, he made his way back to the island paradise to visit the girl on the beach.

Retracing his steps, he swam with even more energy and excitement because knew he would see the girl of his dreams. On the way there, he saw two or three boats using fishing nets and actually catching a lot of fish but also some marine animals. He didn't have time for that. He just kind of bypassed it and swam around the boats as most marine animals do. SeaWalker avoided them because he was on a mission to get to the island to see his girl. But he was curious as to why these boats are there. For now, his mind was on Marina, the girl that he had met and longed to see again. He saw the island in the near distance, and very soon, he crawled up onto the beach and transformed from sea creature to man. He was eagerly looking for the Marina. She was not where she was the day previous, so he continued to journey almost completely to the other side of the island to the small harbor boat and little tiki hut. There, in the distance, he could see the girl with her mother and father sitting at a small table having lunch. SeaWalker didn't know if he should walk up to the family, but he decided to go for it – the calling to see her again feeling so intense. The girl excitedly jumped up from her seat and ran over to SeaWalker and grabbed his hand. "Thank you for coming back. I am very pleased to introduce you to my parents, Harry and Geraldine."

"SeaWalker, it is a pleasure to meet you," said her father who walked out to shake his hand. SeaWalker put his hand out, and the professor grabbed it and gave it a big strong shake. SeaWalker went with it. The mother then came up and gave him a big hug. He was very pleased that the family accepted him right away. The family immediately invited him to sit down and have lunch together. They put a plate in front of SeaWalker and handed him a platter of snapper, a fish that SeaWalker himself had caught from time to time. But this was different. This fish was cooked, but SeaWalker was hungry and decided to go for it. To his surprise, it tasted fantastic! There were also bananas, papayas, mangos and many other fruits. The family was very happy to have SeaWalker visit them and very happy that their daughter had made a new friend. SeaWalker was the type of boy that parents immediately trusted. His eyes were very clear, and he always smiled. He was different to be sure, but he had a sense about him that was good. So, SeaWalker, without even thinking about it, just started grabbing the food with his hands and shoving it into his mouth. He was very hungry. The parents were thinking, Whoa, this kid must be really hungry! But, they figured this was pretty casual; they were on an island. They actually found it quite humorous to watch SeaWalker eat. This kid could really eat they thought. Marina looked at him with wonder, and his smile was contagious, like someone that she could really love and wanted to get to know. The parents were really curious about SeaWalker, but Marina decided that instead of questions from the parents, she would grab SeaWalker and head out for a little boat ride. So the two of them jumped in the little boat. She grabbed the motor, and they cruised off into the harbor then out into the open sea. SeaWalker had never been on one of these boats - at least on the surface. He found it very amusing. Marina was excited by his enthusiasm, so she decided to gun it and go really fast. The little 45-horse engine could really move the little skiff and that made SeaWalker scream with excitement. It danced over the calm waters.

It was a crystal clear day with visibility exceeding over a hundred feet. SeaWalker couldn't resist leaning out over the bow of the boat, looking into the sea and recognizing many of the animals he had come to know in his day-to-day travels. This was a different perspective, however. It was great… just perched up on the bow of the boat as it moved effortlessly along the sea.

*This beautiful new creature mesmerized young SeaWalker like nothing before...*

*W*

# CHAPTER TWENTY-FOUR

## CAPTURED

They raced across the water for some time, and all of a sudden right in front of them, the fishing boats had moved closer to their location. Marina was very concerned about this. In fact, she knew these boats to not only be fishing but capturing dolphins for sea life parks in Asia. These men could be paid very large amounts of money for every wild dolphin they captured. She was very nervous, so she decided to turn the boat around quickly. When she turned, SeaWalker fell off the bow and into the water.

The two fishing boats were dragging a large net between them in order to capture bottlenose dolphins that had been sighted in the area. Before SeaWalker could even transform, he somehow got caught up in the fishing net. The more he struggled, the more tangled he became. He raced to the surface as quickly as he could to get a gasp of air before his transformation from human back to sea creature.

Suddenly, the boats were right on top of him! The fishermen were thinking that they had caught a dolphin. Marina was horrified, and she turned the boat quickly to look for SeaWalker, but she could not see him anywhere. The fisherman were coming in

# CHAPTER TWENTY-FOUR

very, very close and yelling at her to get out of the area, but she was persistent and would not leave. SeaWalker was trapped in the fishing net, it was impossible for him to untangle himself. Marina was terrified, crying and hysterical. Time passed... two minutes... five minutes... ten minutes... and no sign of SeaWalker. The fisherman were again shouting at her to get out of the area. After fifteen minutes, she decided to go back and get her parents. With no sign of SeaWalker anywhere, she feared the worst.

The fishermen were excited. They had finally caught their prize. They felt a tug on the line, and they started to reel in the nets. As the nets were pulled onto the boat, and they saw one small dolphin, and it was placed into the holding tank. SeaWalker was also in the net. He was raised from below the surface and eventually towed up onto the deck of the fishing boat.

All of the fishermen gasped! It was if they had just captured an alien from outer space. This was not a bottlenose dolphin nor a human, but something completely different. After their original shock, they were excited that they had captured something that may be as unique as a mermaid, the first that any of them had ever witnessed or, for that matter, had ever been captured by any fisherman. Their first thought was of money. This creature would be an oddity, something that would bring bids from the by highest bidders from countries around the world! It would be on

# CAPTURED

exhibit and draw millions of people due to its fascination. It was like finding hidden treasure.

SeaWalker was terrified after being all wrapped up in this net. His strength was diminished for he had been fighting for his life. Now, they were pulling him out of the net and placing him in a water tank on the boat, so at that moment, he was really scared he may die. He was also worried about Marina. What had happened to her, and what would she think? But for the time being, he tried to regain his strength and composure. He had to figure out how to get out of this mess.

They put him in the tank and closed the portal, encasing him in this water habitat for transportation. It was a very small tank with not much room for him to move around. He felt like he was in a cage for a wild animal. In fact, that is exactly where he was. Both of the boats came together as they called a third boat. All the crew came together with the Captain, and everyone wanted to see this new animal that they had captured, an animal that must be worth millions of dollars, maybe more.

They couldn't have been more excited and pleased. More than a dolphin, they may have had captured an ocean alien. They were curious themselves about what type of creature this was. They decided to call off the rest of the dolphin chase and head back to the harbor to try and sell this creature to the highest bidder. It was a four-hour boat ride back to Miami, and the first people that were called to the boat were from the Miami Sea Life Park. They couldn't believe the story they heard on their marine radios, and they were quite sure that these mariners were drinking lots of rum and making up some wild fish tale. But still, they were curious to see what had been captured. Was it a different type of whale species or a shark? They were not sure, but they were interested all the same.

The fisherman thought they may have captured the Loch Ness Monster itself! The more they thought about it, the more they thought how much money they were going to make. So, they got on the radio and started calling everyone they knew. In fact, they called the owner, and he too thought they were a little crazy but again… he thought, well what if they did capture something really unique? Big Foot? The Loch Ness Monster? Mermaid, Sea creature. This would be amazing. So, the owner decided to meet them at the dock to have a firsthand look.

For SeaWalker though, it was nothing but fear. He had to get out of there and get to Marina and tell her that he was alright. For Marina, this was the worst thing ever. It was a nightmare. Had her new friend SeaWalker died? Had he drowned? Did he get caught in their fishing net? She was terrified as she raced back to the harbor and up to her parents' hut, screaming. Her parents raced towards her as she told them what had happened to SeaWalker.

The parents jumped into the skiff with Marina to race back to where they were, but the fishing boats were long gone. They trolled the water for hours in a desperate search for SeaWalker. With Marina crying, they made their way slowly back to the island. The seas were calm as the fishermen raced back to Miami. By then, the owner had already called several sea life parks, not only in the United States but in Japan, China – everywhere! Telling them not only that they had been successful in capturing dolphins in the Triangle, but there may also be a possibility that they had captured an animal that was unique, almost a mermaid. Would anyone believe it? Would the owner himself believe it? Time would tell, and the boats would be back in the harbor soon.

Marina and her parents finally made it back to the island, her in tears and her parents in disbelief. The boy that they just met and barely knew was now gone. Marina was terrified. She could not stop crying. Her parents could only put their arms around her to console her, "We can only hope for the best." They had no telephones, no way to communicate. They weren't scheduled to leave the island for at least six weeks. There was really nothing they could do except pray and hope SeaWalker was safe.

# CHAPTER TWENTY-FOUR

On the fishing boats, the fishermen could not stop looking at SeaWalker trying to figure out exactly what they had captured. Was this some type of fish? Some type of man? Maybe both? Was he a merman? Was he some type of species that never had been seen? The Triangle was known for horrific stories, and there were many stories of mermaids and mermen from ancient mariners, but this was something unique. SeaWalker was unwilling to talk. He didn't say a word. He just stayed in one corner of the tank, quietly thinking how he would get out of this situation.

It was night-time when the fishing boat holding SeaWalker arrived at the harbor. There was a holding tank at the nearby sea life park. SeaWalker was transported in the boat's holding tank which had a glass cover and lock. He was transported in the still of the night to the park where he was placed into a larger holding area where they keep dolphins, sea turtles, sea lions and other animals that are captured for display at sea life aquariums. He was transferred from the small holding tank to a larger pool. The fishermen placed SeaWalker in the larger pool and were very proud of them-selves for capturing a creature that promised to collect millions of dollars. They decided to go back to the boat to get a few hours of sleep before the owner arrived early in the morning, leaving SeaWalker in the sea life park holding pool.

As soon as night fell, SeaWalker decided that it was time to go, and he surfaced from the bottom where he had been hiding from the fisherman. He took a look around. His eyes were very good at night, in fact he had night vision. He could see some of the other animals that had been captured; bottlenose dolphins, false killer whales, belugas, little harbor seals and many different types of turtles that he had swam with; loggerheads, greens, ridleys, even the largest leatherback a seven and a half foot giant in a small little bathtub size holding tank.

He was saddened by all of this. He could telepathically hear the animals crying, and in a quick moment, he was out of the tank and walking around the holding area, quickly transforming once again. SeaWalker went around looking into some of the holding tanks. The first one held two white beluga whales, and they immediately surfaced to look at SeaWalker. SeaWalker gazed into their two beautiful, black button eyes and telepathically communicated that he had been captured too and that he was from the sea as well, and he would somehow help rescue them. Their mood changed immediately from sorrow to great happiness, and the affection was mutual as SeaWalker reached out and hugged one of the belugas. The second beluga also came in very close, and SeaWalker wrapped his arms around both of them. All of them had teary eyes. Without thinking or saying a word, there was a special bond, a connection. He reminded them to keep quiet so they wouldn't be noticed.

# CHAPTER TWENTY-FOUR

SeaWalker was starting to realize his purpose for being of the land and the sea. It was to help both worlds. He assured the belugas he would find a way to get them back to the sea and continued to look in some of the other holding tanks. The next tank held several different species of turtles, and the turtles swam right over to SeaWalker, spy hopping their heads out of the water, normally for a breath, but now for a look at their new friend. SeaWalker assured the turtles that he would do everything he could in order to free them from their small cement pens. They asked if he would go over and look at the Leatherback and see how she was doing. SeaWalker moved a few yards away to the small holding tank - barley large enough to encompass the Leatherback. She was captured, a prisoner of this small space where before she had swam free inhabiting and traveling the entire ocean on currents.

SeaWalker had seen a leatherback once. It was amazing looking, traveling weightless in the water world on the Gulf Stream. Their numbers had been depleted and many thought they would soon disappear from the wild ocean. Some leatherbacks were captured for aquariums, a place that was far too small to hold this magnificent animal that was so used to such vast ocean spaces. SeaWalker reached over and grabbed onto a flipper of this beautiful animal, and she sweetly rose her head up and gave him  a little peck on the cheek. He put his cheek up against hers and told her he would be back and do everything he could to get her out of that small tub as soon as possible. SeaWalker didn't want to show it, but he shed a tear after seeing that beautiful animal in such a small environment. It wasn't fair. How could humans do that or for one moment think that was right?

There were many other cement holdings, small, very shallow pools holding a wide variety of marine life from stingrays to sea lions and harbor seals. But as he walked a few steps further, he saw something that just broke his heart. He saw a small group of dolphins in a very shallow cement pool. These were the Atlantic bottlenose dolphins, his family. He raced over to them. Without thinking, he jumped over the cement barrier and into the pool with them. They embraced him from all sides and they communicated, just chattering in the language they both understood. The dolphins had not been this excited for the last few years while they were being held there against their will.

In fact, the dolphins told SeaWalker how they were captured very near the Triangle, very near the island where he had been captured by the same fishermen. They too had been netted and almost drowned, then dragged up onto the boat deck and placed into the small holding tank and then transported here where they have been ever since. Why were they here? Why would anybody do this? He couldn't understand.

# CHAPTER TWENTY-FOUR

But, SeaWalker was determined to find out. He also assured them that he would find them a way home. It was hard for him to stay any longer or he may break down from sadness. He was overcome, but he tried not to show it. He tried to be strong, tried to put on a brave face so they would be confident that he would come back for them. They all embraced once again, and he told them that he had to go to find a way to sea, a way back for them and all the other creatures that were being held captive.

*Behold the new sea creature now captured*
*without truly knowing its place in the Universe...*
                                                    *W*

# CHAPTER TWENTY-FIVE

# ESCAPE

SeaWalker jumped out of the dolphin tank. As he walked into the back area of the sea life park, he noticed large, barbwire electrical fences making it impossible for anybody to get in or out. He also noticed the large doors that entered into the aquarium were locked. It was virtually a prison for aquatic animals. He had to find a way out, and he had to do it quickly.

Many of these animals were not healthy, and their strength had been diminished. Many had all but given up. He had to find the quickest, easiest way to the sea and a way to transport them back to their water home. And it had to happen fast!

He noticed some large pipe tubing. It seemed to be some sort of water filtration system. As he looked over the hillside, he noticed the large pipes, some as large as six foot in diameter, ran straight down to the harbor. Was this a way out? He was not sure, but he followed the pipes all the way back into the facility and eventually he found a large pool that the pipes filled. He also found a valve that allowed water to enter and fill up these large pools with salt water from the harbor. The only way to know for sure was to take a ride down the pipe.

It was scary and dangerous, but he felt if he had any chance of saving himself and the other captured animals, he would have to take the plunge. So he turned the lever. It seemed to open up, and water immediately began filling the pool. Seawalker jumped in, waited for his transformation, and started swimming down through the pipe. It seemed like a long time, but eventually, he came to the end of the pipe. He thrust his way through to open water and immediately sensed that he was in seawater. SeaWalker could immediately taste and smell the natural, pure water of the Atlantic. He swam to the surface and sure enough, from the surface he could see the holding area of the sea life park.

This indeed was an escape route and SeaWalker was not going to waste any time in helping his fellow sea mates escape captivity. The time was now. He reversed his course and swam straight back through the pipe into the pool and immediately went from tank to tank to tank to tank, quickly freeing each of the animals. The belugas were going to be a real challenge. He didn't think that he would be able to get the belugas through the pipes, but he assured them he would find a way. The dolphins could barely make it, but they did. After a couple of hours, he had released every single animal in the holding areas except for the belugas and an orca that had been a prisoner in a tiny cement pool that was not nearly large enough for him. He knew he needed to release the belugas

# ESCAPE

and the orca that he had to find a way. So, he decided to use one of the vehicles for transporting animals. He would somehow get the belugas and orca on the back of the truck and drive through the fence, down the hill, and down to bay where the all could actually swim off the back of the truck!

This was very dangerous, and he knew he was taking a chance. To complicate matters, he had never driven a car before, no matter he thought. He may in fact kill these animals, but after they talked, these animals felt it was worth it. SeaWalker backed the transport vehicle up and, jumped in the pool to helped the large orca whale wiggle on board. Then the two belugas pushed in next to the orca. After the three animals wiggled as far up as they could with their flukes sticking out, SeaWalker jumped into the front seat and released the brakes shifted into gear and rolled through the fence. Down the hill they went... in a trek that could be compared to a Nantucket sleigh ride. It wasn't far, but it sure was hairy.

The truck hit the water! It made a huge splash and a huge sound. The sun was just starting to come up. The owners and the fishermen were starting to arrive at the park at the very moment the truck hit the water. It didn't sink immediately. It took a couple of minutes. The back end sank below the surface and the orca and belugas wiggled themselves off as SeaWalker joined them.

# CHAPTER TWENTY-FIVE

SeaWalker spy hopped above the surface to take one last look and he noticed the owner and fishermen angrily shaking their fists and yelling and running towards the truck that had now been deposited into the harbor.

Ironically, the animals that had been freed earlier waited until SeaWalker got back with the whales and together, they excitedly swam out of the mouth of the harbor into the open sea. It was a joyous moment as they nervously looked across at each other, flipper to flipper, eye to eye… together and free again at last!

As the animals raced back to the open sea, they huddled together for one moment holding hands and flippers in a circle of life. They were so grateful that SeaWalker came and helped them. But many were still concerned that some of the others were left behind, some of them relatives, some of them friends. Some of them had been there many, many years, some over twenty years old. Other aquariums held so many species of fish and other marine animals. One held a very rare giant red octopus that only had a few months to live.

There were many more animals, and SeaWalker promised them he would try and help, but for now, they were finally free and heading home.

SeaWalker, of course, had to get back to Marina to let her know that he was safe and alive! He bid farewell to the other animals and told them he looked forward to seeing them all again. They thanked him and thanked him and thanked him as he raced towards the small island to see the girl on the beach.

*Over exploitation of our ocean life is at a tipping*
*point, some species may never recover...*
*W*

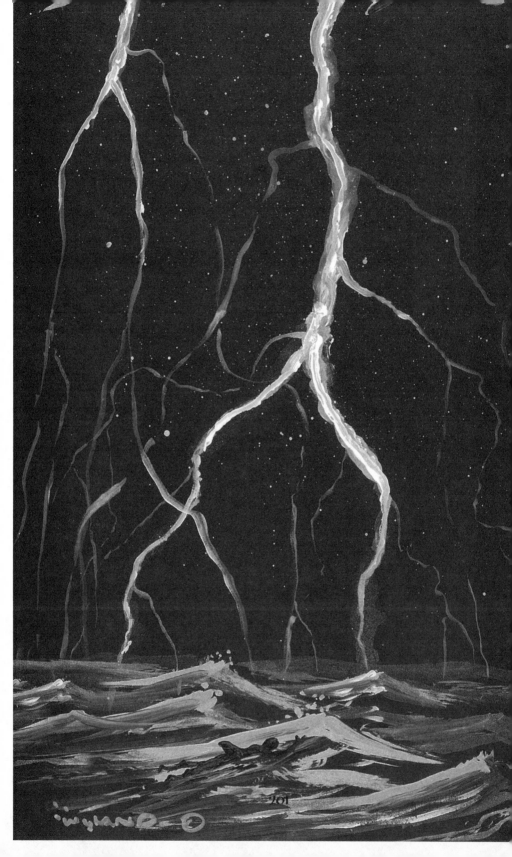

# CHAPTER TWENTY-SIX

# I AM SEAWALKER

SeaWalker raced back to the island to assure the girl on the beach, his one true love, that he was alive and well, and to tell her of his true identity. It took him many hours, but he finally reached the island the next day. As he approached, he saw the small skiff from a distance. He decided to investigate and see Marina was there. As he approached, he heard her crying. She was sitting alone on the skiff. Her head was down and, she was crying softly. He did not wish to startle her, but he swam up to the skiff popping his head up and saying, "Marina, Marina." She thought she was hearing things or dreaming and ignored it at first. Finally, he yelled, "Marina, its me, SeaWalker!" She could not believe her eyes. Her face immediately illuminated with tears of joy as he embraced her.

"SeaWalker, its you! I can't believe its you! You're alive!"

"Yes, its me! I have to tell you something. I must tell you. It's so important!"

"Not now! I am just so happy to see you, happy you're here, happy they didn't get you, happy you didn't drown, and you're really here, so pleased that you are still alive."

"Yes, I am alive but... but... but..."

"Where did you come from? How did you get here?"

"That is what I have to tell you," SeaWalker said, "There is so much I need to tell you. I need to talk to you."

"I need to tell you something."

"Get in the boat," Marina said. "Get in the boat and let me take you home. You must be tired."

"Before I get in the boat, I need to tell you something. It is a secret. Can you keep a secret?"

"Yes. Anything. Please!"

"I am not only SeaWalker. I am also Walker. I am part sea and part man."

"What do you mean? What are you talking about?"

"It's going to be really hard for you to believe this, but my parent's boat sank, and I was taken down to the deep abyss where the gases sustained me. I was transformed as a baby to half human and half marine mammal. I was raised by dolphins. I know it is impossible to believe, but I hope you believe me when I tell you this."

Marina looked at him puzzled, and said, "I believe you. I do! I do!"

She reached out to hug him, and they embraced for a long time. Finally, SeaWalker said, "I don't want you to be scared. When I come out of the water, I am a normal boy. But when I am in the water, I am a sea creature. I can breathe under water. I have gills. Look right here." He turned his head, and she could see his gills under his ears. She was astonished but very happy – thrilled to know that her friend was something special. She knew he was special. She felt it from the very beginning, and now, he was sharing his life with her. She was so proud!

SeaWalker said, "You must keep this secret. If anybody were to find out, I would be a freak. I would be captured and put on display in some aquarium. I must be free to do things for my friends in the sea and on land, so we must keep this our secret."

Marina assured him that she would. She just wanted him to get out of the water and in the boat. SeaWalker said, "Okay, but I don't want you to freak out." He hoisted himself up, and she could see how unique and different he was. He was very large and full. He had a large dorsal fin. His fingers were long and webbed, and his feet were fins. He was really incredible looking. She loved the sea and all the animals of the sea and now had a friend that was both. She watched in astonishment at the transformation as he slowly began to dry off. She couldn't believe her eyes. It was magical. It was like a mirage.

She watched the whole process and smiled deeply and said, "I will keep this secret forever."

He believed her, but for now, they needed to get back to land. He had so much he wanted to share with her, so much to tell her. He wanted to tell her of the capture and of the release of the other animals and the need to get back in order to release the rest.

It was a short boat ride to the island. By then, SeaWalker had transformed. He was human. As they came up on the beach, her parents ran eagerly to them both happily yelling, "He's alive! He's alive! Are you okay? What happened?"

SeaWalker assured them he was fine and that everything was going to be alright. He was just happy to be back... and he was hungry!

"That's great 'cause we just made a bunch iconic and island food over here, and you are welcome to have dinner with us SeaWalker."

So, they put their arms around him, and they all walked arm in arm back to the small hut and had a tremendous Caribbean dinner around a beautiful campfire. Of course, SeaWalker could not stop looking at Marina. He was so pleased that she knew his secret and would keep it forever.

It soon became night, and the parents invited SeaWalker to stay. He agreed. They gave him a sleeping bag, and Marina took hers and they camped out right in front of the fire watching the night sky. Neither one could sleep. SeaWalker was far too excited and happy to be alive and able to talk. He just lovingly looked at her, and they both looked at the sky and watched shooting stars all night. They thought about the next day when they would share all their stories, all their adventures and the future they would have together.

As the sun rose, SeaWalker and Marina got up. They grabbed some orange juice and a couple of papayas and decided to go for a walk on the beach to talk about all the events that had happened. Marina was very excited to hear about how he had escaped the

# CHAPTER TWENTY-SIX

fishermen, and SeaWalker told her in detail. It was an unbelievable story. SeaWalker believed that he was good and that good was on his side, and with a friend like Marina, he could accomplish anything he dreamed of. His dream was to bridge the worlds of the sea and land and to bring people together. He wanted to help them see that every person is connected to every sea creature and all life was important and equal and that we must not destroy any life. There was a balance that absolutely had to be maintained on our water planet, and some humans and sea creatures are predators and others are protectors. The ocean was considered by its inhabitants to be one ocean, one nation. It needed more protectors according to SeaWalker, good souls to protect our land and sea!. There was plenty of bounty there. Of course, people and fish had to eat, but there was a chain of life that had to be maintained, and the future needed a new paradigm. SeaWalker felt strongly that he could play a role. Marina felt strongly that she could support him and also play a role. Together, they could change the world. They had big dreams. Watching the shooting stars all night, they made many promises and had many dreams and many wishes, all for others and not themselves. SeaWalker continued to tell her the story of his capture and how easy it was to escape and how the other animals had asked him to help them. For some reason, everything fell into place, but he was still upset that other animals were still there. He wanted to find a way to release them. He had assured the animals that he would be back.

He asked Marina if she would go with him. She eagerly agreed. "I could be a huge asset. I have been to these parks many times since I was a child. I know every aquarium and every habitat and all the animals that live there. Let's go for it. Let's get there and free those animals so they can get back to their ocean homes."

Both agreed. They now had to devise a way to get off the island and back to the sea life park to accomplish their mission. They decided to get together when Marina returned with her family to South Florida in the next few weeks. She lived in Ft. Lauderdale, and that was only about an hour away from Miami.

They would have plenty of time to plan the rescue. In the meantime, they were grateful to be together, and they spent the whole day holding hands and thinking about how great it will be to be rejoined in South Florida. SeaWalker was also eager to get back to the tribe to tell them that he had released some of the dolphins that had disappeared from the Triangle. Would they believe his story? Time would tell.

After spending the day with Marina, SeaWalker made his way back to the tribe, back to his home under the sea. He was pretty tired from all the excitement. When he got back, he quietly snuck into his cavern and just laid at the surface for hours and hours and hours. When he woke up, many of his dolphin friends were eager to see him and asked him where he had been and what happened. He said, "If I told you, you probably wouldn't believe me." They said, "Yes we would, yes we would, tell us!" So, he gathered all of his friends together, along with the crab, and they huddled together. He began telling the incredible story of the girl on the beach and being captured by the fishermen, the walkers, and being taken to a holding tank and seeing the many different animals, including some of the other dolphin tribe members that were captured.

The dolphins, of course, were fascinated and angry that these walkers would do such a thing. SeaWalker had caught them red handed, and they now had proof. They cheered and cheered. In fact, they made so much noise, the elders swam in. SeaWalker had to repeat the entire story! They looked at SeaWalker in admiration and said,

"You are a brave soul," and "Thank you for saving our brothers and sisters."

SeaWalker said, "It was nothing. Anybody would do it."

He also said he was happy, but he wasn't done. He had to go back. They were nervous about that and asked him if he was sure,

"We don't think that's a good idea. What if they capture you and put you on display permanently?" He said that was a chance he was willing to take, and he alone had to take it. But he felt strongly that he could make a difference. He had already been there once. The elders were concerned that the walkers would wait for him. But he assured them that everything would be fine and that he had a friend who knew the aquarium intimately and would help him achieve his goal of freeing all the animals, large and small, so they could swim freely again. The elders knew they couldn't change his mind and embraced him and wished him well.

*SeaWalker came into existence at a time*
*when humans threatened all life on the planet...*
                                                        *W*

# CHAPTER TWENTY-SEVEN

# RETURN TO THE SEA

Se aWalker left the Triangle, and he headed east for Ft. Lauderdale in South Florida to rendezvous with Marina. She and her parents lived on a nice boat in the harbor. It was not too far from the Miami Sea Life Park. They were to rendezvous in the evening, just after sundown, and together head towards the sea life park to release the remaining animals in the aquarium.

SeaWalker arrived to the boat dock to meet Marina right around 7:30 pm, and of course, she was waiting for him. As he surfaced, she was at the end of the dock excitedly waving at him. They embraced for a long time without saying a word, excited to see each other after so many weeks apart and so excited to finally go back to the sea life park and try to help these animals in captivity. Marina had a smaller boat, a little zodiac, and she helped SeaWalker climb aboard. It was dark so nobody could see his transformation, but the moon was starting to rise. Marina could see the exciting transformation. She loved seeing this and was amazed every time it happened. SeaWalker was a little embarrassed, but he had brought some board shorts and a towel this time. She turned around for his privacy.

# CHAPTER TWENTY-SEVEN

Without hesitation, they headed the boat out of the harbor and along the inter-coastal and headed for Miami. It was a couple hours trip, and they chatted about what's been happening since they last saw each other, but mostly, they were very excited to do something for all the animals at the sea life park.

Before long, they arrived at their destination. They pulled the zodiac right up to the edge of the harbor where they could see the seawater pipe where SeaWalker had released many of the captive animals on his first trip. They tied the boat off down at the end of the small dock and gazed up at the park which just closed a few hours earlier. But, it seemed like there was a lot of security, big men in uniforms carrying guns. Many people were walking around the area now... probably due to the fact that SeaWalker previously released many of the animals. To the normal eye, Marina and SeaWalker just looked like two kids hanging out on the dock, and that was good. It was to their advantage. Nobody would expect teenage kids to break into a sea life aquarium and release hundreds of animals!

The security guard was sipping on a little whiskey, a little Jack. He was half asleep and half drunk. He looked up at the aquarium, and when he saw SeaWalker's face, he was absolutely in shock. He looked at SeaWalker and looked down at the Jack Daniels bottle, then back up at SeaWalker and back down at the bottle. He decided to put the bottle into the garbage and that he needed to quit drinking. He thought he was seeing some sort of mirage, so he started rubbing his eyes really hard, and by this time, SeaWalker was already gone to the next exhibit. SeaWalker made his way from one tank to the next, to the next, to the next assuring everybody that they were going to all leave together. He told them he would open all the valves and everybody needed to swim out to the harbor and then out to the open sea. He added, the only way this would work was if everybody worked together and nobody rushed to scramble out. They all had to be in sync, and everybody agreed. Even the sharks were on board – even the beautiful sand tiger sharks with their big toothy grins. So, females and children would go first, followed by the rest into the tube and taking the ride out to the harbor. When they reached the harbor, everybody need to swam toward the open ocean and into the currents to their home. It sounded easy, and SeaWalker was ready to implement the escape plan.

Amazingly, it went like clockwork. They all started moving towards the back tanks through the main pipe, and SeaWalker led the way. He was like a cheerleader, praising and helping as some of the animals were very weak. All of the other animals were all helping too. They were working to push each other towards the exit pipe. Everyone had waited for so long for this moment – when they would return to the open sea. It was very emotional for many of the animals. It was happening really quickly as they were pushed through the pipe and into the bay. In a matter of two and a half hours, every single fish and mammal, along with some of the sea otters who decided it was time to go, cruised right out of the pipe and into the bay. After three hours, the entire aquarium was empty, and SeaWalker was ready to leave! But before he left, he took a look back and thought, I never want to see another sea animal here again.

All of a sudden, he decided to sabotage the place! When the last animal escaped, he turned all the pumps to flow a certain way so the entire aquarium would be flooded - he went around and opened up all the flood pipes and flooded the entire building. He headed for the pipe finally. He took a Nantucket-type sleigh ride down and out to the sea. He was the last man out, or sea creature in this case. Either way, it was fine with him. As he made his way down the pipe, like riding a waterslide, he couldn't help smiling and laughing hysterically.

His plan had worked. He had rescued all these fish and animals and returned them to the sea. Marina was also excited as she ran down the hill trying not to make too much noise. All of a sudden, alarms started sounding, and there was lots of commotion. Windows were breaking, and security guards were waving their arms and screaming. The seawater had indeed flooded the entire building! SeaWalker and Marina would celebrate later. For now, they had to get the heck out of there, so they both jumped in the boat and headed back to Ft. Lauderdale... grinning widely as they raced north!

*Ancient dog-like mammals left the land,*
*walking into the sea for food and a new life*
*never to return...*

*W*

# CHAPTER TWENTY-EIGHT

# OCEAN CELEBRATION

As the zodiac raced back to Ft. Lauderdale, away from the scene of the victory, SeaWalker sat with his arms around Marina lovingly gazing at her from time to time, appreciating her courage and her desire to help him save the animals of the sea. It was very gratifying for both of them, and they couldn't help letting out a little snicker here and there. They had actually outsmarted the walkers, and all the animals were heading back to their families for a reunion.

One day, they would have an ocean celebration, a summit where all the animals could come together and tell their stories and talk about how they could do more to help each other. For many years, the animals of the sea thrived, but now, they had one enemy. That was man. But were they all like that? Were they all out to destroy them? SeaWalker didn't think so. He felt, like Marina, there were many that were good. He was always looking at the positive side, the good side. He felt that good and evil both existed in the world and that good would one day overcome the evil. He also felt that he had an important role to play in bringing the good in the ocean and the good on land together so that they could live as one.

# CHAPTER TWENTY-EIGHT

After a couple of hours, they returned safely to Marina's parents' boat. She was exhausted and hugged SeaWalker who assured her that he would see her again soon on the island. She would know he was there. He would send a sign. He didn't really tell her what it would be, but she would know. He hugged her goodbye, a long embrace. They looked at each other with big smiles, and she waved him goodbye as he jumped into the sea and raced back home to his family in the Triangle.

SeaWalker finally made it back to the Triangle, He heard a loud noise in the distance, lots of animals in celebration. As he got closer, he realized the celebration was for him. The elders had called all of the sea animals in the area together to celebrate the victory, the release of all the sea creatures in captivity at the aquarium. SeaWalker received a hero's welcome! He was a little embarrassed by the whole thing, but he was happy to see all of his family together with big smiles. He also saw a lot of the animals he released from the aquarium. It appeared that the ocean was a small neighborhood. Word spread fast on the conch shell telegraph about this new creature that had helped save the many species of animals that inhabited the waters of the Atlantic.

All of the animals that were rescued and safely returned to their families had been speaking of SeaWalker, and now it was time for the guest of honor to say a few words. The elders called him up. SeaWalker was a little uneasy at first. He was a creature of very few words. He just looked out at everyone and got a little teary and said, "I am very happy that I am part of this family and that I could do a small part to help return everyone to their families. It means so much to Marina and I, and I just hope we can do more. I hope we can come together, both the walkers and the animals of the sea like us, to try and protect this beautiful ocean planet for many years to come. I am sure we have much more in common than we have differences, and I hope one day that we can come together and have an ocean treaty that gives each of us the promise of hope and inspiration... so that we can live in peace and help each other enjoy the bounty of the land and sea. Thank you everyone. I need to get some sleep!" With roaring applause, flippers flapping, tails slapping and everyone embracing, SeaWalker headed slowly towards his resting place at the surface, where he would float and dream of the last few weeks.

*Whales have no enemies, God save man...*

*W*

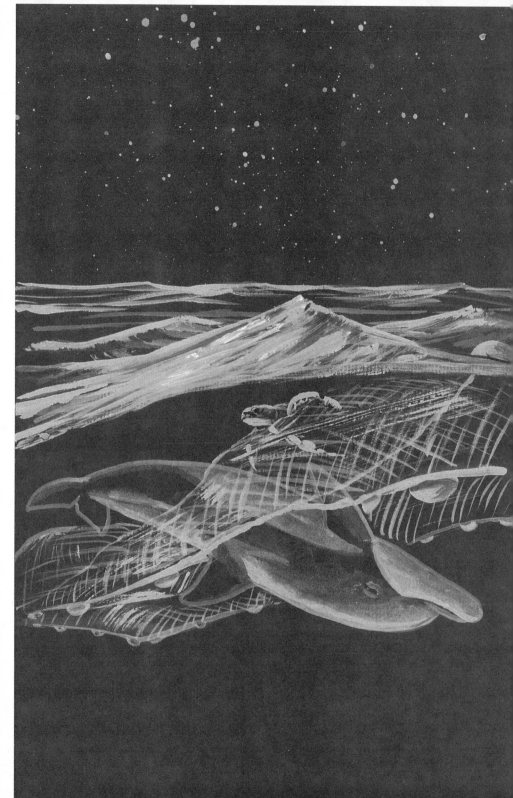

# CHAPTER TWENTY-NINE

# REVENGE OF THE SEA

**S**eaWalker awoke after another very long sleep to a rally that began as a homecoming and was now a full-fledged protest against the humans, the walkers. Word spread quickly throughout the Atlantic and beyond on the ocean currents telegraph.

All the creatures of the sea decided to join together in an ocean alliance to deal with the humans who had been destroying their world for over a hundred years. It was now time to take a stand. To the humans, the animals were just dumb creatures to be used as resources. These fish, these turtles, these whales belonged to them. But the marine animals saw it differently. They were there first. They had been in the oceans for millions of years before humans crawled into the ocean and then back onto land from mud puddles. The marine animals were dignified, though. They never looked at themselves as superior. In fact, they believed every living soul was important and vital for the continuation of all species, even the humans. But... the animals of the sea had enough! They stood by and watched their home being poisoned and over-fished and destroyed in every imaginable way, and it was time to stand up against these tyrants!!

# CHAPTER TWENTY-NINE

So, what began as a homecoming and celebration for SeaWalker had now become a rallying point for many many animals which became a huge summit. The elders took a leading role. Dolphins were respected because of their positive attitude and family values and the idea that they never took more than they needed and always gave back. The dolphins were considered one of the most intelligent beings, not only in the animal kingdom but throughout the Universe. The elders decided it was time to put together a coalition to finally give the walkers a taste of their own medicine.

So, the dolphin elders got together and one by one decided they had enough. They watched too many of their brothers, sisters and children over generations be taken or killed and exploited in numerous ways. They had enough, and they were not going to take it any more. But what would they do? They decided that they would turn the tides at every opportunity, and every animal that had been exploited by humans would now take a stand. They would, for the first time, not be hunted or destroyed. They would not allow the poison to enter their home. They would not allow any more animals to be captured – from the largest whale to the smallest fish. They would not allow these monsters to fire harpoons into their backs. They were done playing nice,, and it was time to put the centuries of man's conquest of the sea to an end... once and for all.

# REVENGE OF THE SEA

After all of the dolphin elders spoke, it was time for some of the other animals to speak. The greatest and largest animals of all the underwater kingdom came to the podium to speak next.

The blue whales had been hunted to the point that 90% of their population had been destroyed. In fact, they were having trouble finding each other in the empty oceans. Many years ago, their sounds would travel over 100 miles, but now, with all of the boat noise and their diminished numbers, they were having trouble finding each other. Their populations were at such low levels that they may never recover. The king of the blue whale tribe spoke first, "We have evolved over the last fifty million years. We have quietly stood by and watched our brothers and sisters be hunted for no good reason. We have not once harmed any human, but they continued to kill us. We agree with the summit that it is time to take a stand before the last whale is hunted. We are with you completely. We are, of course, the largest and considered by many the gentlest creatures of the sea. But not anymore. We have been pushed to far, and it is time for us to take action. Be assured that all of us will be on the hunt for any ship that takes aim at any of our families. Never again will we allow this to happen. We will ram and sink them all. Thank you."

Now it was time for the orcas, who were considered the top

predator of all the oceans of all the world, to speak. They were chomping at the bit to be heard. Their leader, a large male named Sharkbite, came up to the podium. "We too have watched and stood by as our family members were captured and put into small pools to be on display for human enjoyment. We have forgiven humans for many, many years, but it is now time for us to take a stand. We will not stand by and watch as they continue to capture our brothers and sisters. The ocean war is on! The ocean is ours. They can have their land, but the ocean is ours. And when they enter our home, they will be dealt with severely. We are very strong indeed, but we only take what we need to survive. We are conscious to never take more and have always left enough so that they could prosper. But the humans are greedy, and it is time for them to learn a life lesson. If we have to take the lead and show them the way, we will. We stand united, and we support all of our ocean friends and families in this battle to once again claim our territories - which have no nations and no borders."

One by one, representatives from all the underwater animal kingdom spoke. The blue fin tuna, even the sea turtles, who were very quiet and normally floated around the ocean currents minding their own business, got involved. One of the large loggerheads approached the podium. He said, "We have been hunted and destroyed for food and gift products and for every single reason imaginable, and we are tired of it! We have tried to avoid the humans. We even befriended some of the ones that wear funny facemasks and blow bubbles in the sea. But it is now time for all turtles to come together and join the ocean alliance and stop these predators once and for all. We commend this meeting of the ocean minds, and we look forward to joining you in this campaign."

Even the small damsel fish, which many of the humans consider small but very mean (it has been said that if they were larger, even a foot, no human would ever enter the water) decided to take their aggression even further and become the piranhas of the sea and not allow these humans one opportunity to destroy their water world. They were mad as heck, and they were not going to take it any more either. After the damsels, a small puffer fish came up to the stand. He said that he had heard the millions of his brothers and sisters were taken, killed and filled with air so that they could be some sort of window displays in restaurants. This was totally unacceptable. How would a human like to be taken and killed and blown-up and then hung in a window under the sea? This was a horrible act, and they were now ready to join in and help save not only the puffers but all fish, large and small…even the whales too.

After seven or eight hours, many of the animal species had voiced their opinions. All of them had a horror story to tell about how humans had decimated their kind. Not one animal wanted to continue the status quo. They all agreed that their stand needed to happen as soon as possible. At the end, all of the representatives of the tribes spoke once again.

"We are speaking with one voice. Beginning tomorrow, we will never allow the walkers to take advantage of our kind. Every act will be met with force. They will know our power and numbers. We may lose a lot of our kind in this campaign, but it will be worth it for our families in the future. So, let's everybody put our heads down and pray for peace, but if we can't achieve peace … then we will enlist all of the ocean forces to take on these predators."

This was met with loud cheering. All of the voices of the sea! It sounded like underwater thunder. "So it is agreed," the elders finally said, "We are an ocean alliance until all of this stops and we create a sea change in this century, that will impact all of our lives for many generations to come!"

After a long, long sleep, SeaWalker awoke to two of his dolphin friends shaking him to tell him of the ocean alliance. He was a little groggy, and he started to comprehend what all this meant. The sea animals, gentle for so long, living in harmony and knowing that the humans were powerful and could seek revenge were largely ignored and avoided at all cost. But what he was hearing really scared him. He knew this was a declaration of war and this meant a lot more animals, his friends, might die. But, he understood. He saw firsthand how the humans had destroyed many of the fish populations, captured dolphins, killed whales and many other atrocities. It didn't take him too long to decide which side to be on. He would be on the side of the sea. He would not stand by and watch the humans destroy the planet.

As he swam around the Triangle, it was as if everyone was smiling and anticipating what was going to happen. SeaWalker was a little apprehensive, but he really liked and enjoyed that everyone was together, pulling in the same direction. What would happen first? Who would be the first to draw blood if that's what it came to? It didn't take very long to find out.

Indeed, first blood was drawn! A large sports fishing boat had been bill fishing in the Triangle. The previous day, instead of tagging and releasing, these guys kept every single fish, including the small ones. But now it was time for the billfish to get their revenge. A large marlin decided he would set the bait. He came up behind the boat and the fishermen got very excited. Just to tease them, he did a large breach above the water while doing a spinning maneuver. They thought they had a chance to catch the big one, but instead, the marlin raced up to the boat and jumped up along side the fishermen, scaring one of them up out of his chair. Without a moment's notice, he leaped from the side of the boat, spearing the fisherman right in the buttocks.

The fisherman screamed bloody murder as the others looked on in horror. "That had to hurt," SeaWalker thought. "Boy, that had to hurt." After spearing the fisherman in the butt, he wiggled off the back of the boat and back into the sea without any harm to himself but plenty of harm and embarrassment to the fishermen. It was a severe blow, not only to the buttocks, but also to their dignity. Instead of continuing the hunt, they had to return to South Florida and visit the emergency room where they could sew up his left cheek.

Well strike one up, one win for the fish! Fish one, humans zero. All over the oceans there were similar stories. As far as Alaska, stories were coming in of the king crabs. After being trapped in the cages, hundreds of them rushing out of the cages, snapping onto the fishermen's ears, noses, anything they could grab. The fishermen were so scared that they ended up releasing all of the king crabs and making a beeline back to their home ports. As far away as Japan, where the whalers in Taiji were driving pilot whales into a small cove so they could be cut up and sold to the fish markets. The whales had another idea; they had another plan. As the fishing boats chased them, the whales decided to do the chasing. Over four-dozen pilot whales turned and headed straight at the whaling boats, capsizing them, ramming them and knocking the fishermen into the water. Ironically, many of the fishermen could not swim. The pilot whales grabbed their feet and dragged them down to Davy Jones' locker. The pilot whales, it seemed, had been hunted every year, and much of their family had been so hunted and destroyed that they had virtually no chance to recover. The Japanese even decided that they would kill the smaller whales. But not this time! They had enough! So, by the time they were done, all of the small fishing boats were on the bottom of the sea. And, for the fish and reefs, it provided another sanctuary. But one thing was for sure, the ocean animals had decided it was time to take a stand. Even the Native Americans that had recently began hunting whales again were to encounter a different kind of friendly gray whale. Instead of the gray whales coming over to curiously check out the small fishing boats and then being slaughtered, they swam at these fishing boats at break-neck speed, ramming these boats and sinking them to the bottom. The gray whales could not find it in their hearts to kill any of these people, but they sent them a strong message! The fishermen swam back to the shore in fear screaming, "These are not the gentle giants. These are not the gentle giants!"

Even the gentlest, slow moving sea creatures, the manatees, sought revenge after many years of being run over by boat motors. They had enough! They decided that they were going to get even this time. The gentle manatees decided that they would go to the bottom and remove some of the larger logs and float them up right in front of the speeding boats. This of course, created havoc as dozens and dozens of boats lost their motors and propellers, and some even sank. The manatees won. It was a good day for ocean inhabitants.

As promised, the orcas decided it was time to take a stand. The orca tribes located off of the coast of Iceland were hunted by orca merchants for over forty years, so many of these families had a member taken. Usually, the younger family members were taken; they were easier to capture and sell to the highest bidders from marine life parks around the world. But, not now! The largest orca pod was hunting their herring when they heard a sound from a long distance, It was one of the familiar boats that had come there annually to take a few members of their family. So, they decided instead of running away, they would charge them at full speed and try to capture a human. The entire tribe raced toward one of the capture boats and rammed it from the side. One of the crew fell into the water. The orcas grabbed his pant legs and dragged him down about forty feet. They holded him there as he feared for his life. The orcas came right over to his face and stared at him and gave him a growl. Before he drowned, they quickly took him to the surface.

After he caught a breath of air, they grabbed him by the back of the shirt and swam off with him for many miles. The other crew members were terrified and wanted nothing more to do with this hunt. All they wanted to do was find their missing crew member, but to no avail. The orcas, for the first time, had taken an aggressive stand. The humans decided that this was something they had to think about. The orcas were smart enough to know they could not kill this human, but they could certainly frighten him to the extent he would never want to enter these waters again. That is exactly what they did! They put the fear of orca into this man, hoping he would tell the others. They took him to a nearby shoreline after roughing him up a bit and dumped him on the beach. They then returned him back to the boat and chased the boat out of the area for good.

All around the world, in every ocean and every waterway, the marine life was chasing the humans out of their environment. Before a net even hit the water, angry marine animals of all sizes and shapes were moving together on the humans. They put the fear of the ocean into these walkers, and the ocean creatures were relentless. Every single boat and every single human that entered the water environment was chased out and away from the fishing grounds. It was a phenomenon that was happening, not only in the Triangle, but also in every water habitat on the planet.

# CHAPTER TWENTY NINE

The whole world was buzzing about sea animals seeking revenge. The discussions were in all the media and in every town and coffee shop was, "Oh my God! These animals are angry!" And the solutions were all over the board. Some humans were angry and wanted to kill everything. Some said, "Hey, it's about time these animals stuck up for themselves." And everybody wanted something to happen. But the United States top scientist and head of the scientific board for NOAA was an ocean advocate and had a hunch that something needed to change. For many years, he had based his theory on pure science; but now it was more than just science. It was the soul of the sea and the intelligence of the sea. It was something that really went against pure science. He was never considered a pure scientist - but one who thought a little deeper and was a little more of a visionary. He actually saw both sides, the sea animals' side and the human's side. He was a very diplomatic guy and understood the exploitation of the sea. For many years, he had lobbied with the United Nations to call attention to man's destruction of the fishing stocks, whaling and many other issues. He was well respected. He, of course, was the person the entire world looked to for vision. What should humans do now?

Dr. Goodfellow was the head of the United Ocean Alliance and ambassador for the United Nations Ocean Resources. Dr.

# REVENGE OF THE SEA

Goodfellow was somebody that, like Jacques Cousteau in the 20th Century, commanded a great deal of respect. He had spent his entire life as a marine biologist and as a diver. He was an artist, a painter of marine life. But, he was also the highest-ranking official on ocean matters and policy. What would he do now that the oceans were striking back? He held a press conference at the United Nations where he assured everyone that the sea was in peril! Even the sharks were in trouble. Over 90% of their populations had diminished. The balance of the sea had been disturbed, maybe permanently. The sea, it seemed, was taking revenge. He wondered why it took this long. But, he thought maybe the sea and its inhabitants had been pushed to the brink. He tried to humanize the animals. His message was that all humans needed to reflect on the damage they had caused. Why wouldn't these animals seek revenge? Why wouldn't they be angry? And where did humans get off thinking they were the only beings that deserved to rule the planet? Particularly, since they had only been part of the marine world in the last few thousand years.

At the press conference, Dr. Goodfellow was amazed at how much hostility was out there. Even the media and reporters were hostile. It seemed like everyone had a story of the animals affecting the humans. And Dr. Goodfellow, although he was trying to be apolitical, finally slammed his hand on the pedestal and said, "We all need to understand the damage that has been caused, some of it irreversible. I'm with you on much of what you are saying, but you need to appreciate the intelligence of some of these creatures that inhabit the oceans. We are short time visitors in their world. We cannot continue to keep on taking, taking, taking without suffering the consequences. I am not sure why all these animals are acting this way. My only guess is that they have been pushed to the limits, and they are angry with us." At the end of the press conference, a hand was raised by a young man in the very back of the room and the marine biologist called on him to speak. He did not know this young man but felt strongly that it was time to hear from our younger generation. When called, SeaWalker stood up and every head turned, "Sir, you are exactly right. The undersea world has been pushed to this extreme. Generally, a peaceful under water society, it has now decided that it must take a stand if it is going to survive. The humans must change their ways. They must stop taking animals from the sea for their own selfish reasons. It is time they respect life in the sea and on land. There needs to be a new period, an environmental renaissance century in history where humans and animals have mutual respect for each others' lives." SeaWalker continued, "I may be young, but I understand much of the undersea world."

Many of these animals are like family to me, and I want to see them live and prosper without the interference of man. I hope, sir, that you can communicate with humans all over the globe. They only want to be left alone so that they can survive and take care of their families like we do here. They have reached the breaking point, sir. They are not asking for anything from humans, except to be left alone so they can live and prosper in a peaceful ocean world."

The professor nodded his head in agreement and everyone looked puzzled. Who was this young man? Why did he speak with such clarity and honesty? The cameras were pointed at him and came in close on his eyes and face. He became a symbol for a whole generation of young people who shared his concern. "What is your name?" The professor asked him. "Young man, what is your name?" He said, "My name is simply SeaWalker, sir. And thank you for taking the time to listen to me." The professor thanked him profusely and said that he would convene the world's top scientists and policymakers in the next few days so they could have a summit to create a new ocean alliance of leaders who saw the ocean not as a product to exploit, but as a product to restore and give back to its original natives: the fish, whales, turtles and all aquatic animals of the undersea nation, a nation with no borders. And with that, the press conference ended and SeaWalker slipped out the back door and made his way back to the New York harbor and Hudson River into the sea where he would report back to the tribal leaders in the Triangle.

The next day, SeaWalker called a meeting with the elders to explain some of the new information he had received. The elders were amazed at how easily SeaWalker could slip into the walkers' world and back into theirs. Indeed, the prophecies that were expressed when SeaWalker was rescued about him somehow being the key to combining both the above and below worlds was coming true indeed. SeaWalker explained that a very important man had a vision for building the first ocean alliance bringing together all people and all nations to protect the rights of the ocean nation... all sea animals from the smallest minnows to the largest whales. He felt that this man had the foresight and courage to stand up for them. SeaWalker was optimistic that things would change. Now, it was time to ask all animals of the sea to meet again. They had made a statement that was heard around the globe, and it was time for all the animals of the sea to go back to their peaceful nature and give the humans a chance to respond. That is what they did. History had shown that the animals of the ocean kingdom were very forgiving, and now that they had raised their voices for the first time, they might see their old ways restored and mend the damage that had been done over the last century. Most of it done by one predator – man.

*Man's killing of the largest creatures to inhabit the earth was unthinkable...*

*W*

# CHAPTER THIRTY

# JOURNEY TO THE ABYSS

After only a few weeks, the world had completely changed. The revolt against the humans had a profound impact and newer, brighter ideas took hold. Finally, there was an environmental renaissance brewing, and the call to save the planet was on the minds of all 8 billion humans - in every country and in every city of the world. It was finally time for a global ocean Bill of Rights! For SeaWalker though, it was time for him to continue his quest. Since his rescue and throughout his entire life, he had thought about where he came from and what happened to his parents. He decided, from the bits and pieces he was able to collect, that he was rescued as a baby from a sunken boat. He concluded that he would be able to estimate the area where the boat may have gone down in the storm. His instincts were pretty good, he thought. He had surveyed most of the Triangle, but there was one part of the ocean where dolphins couldn't go. It was the deepest part of the abyss. He felt he was now old enough and strong enough to make the journey.

He meditated at the surface for nearly a half hour taking in deep breaths. He was preparing for his deepest dive ever... into the dark abyss hoping to find the boat that went down in the storm, taking his parents lives. Now, he was ready. He started to descend into the deep canyons. 200 feet... 400... 600... 1,000... 2,000.... 3,000 feet deep where no dolphin had ever gone. He wasn't sure if he was designed for this deep water, but he felt fine and continued to descend. His body squished like the sperm whales that hunt for giant squid in the deep ocean. It was nearly pitch black, but he had night vision and echolocation. He could see some of the phosphorescent creatures, weird creatures of every size and dimension, many curious about why SeaWalker was down there. Deeper and deeper he descended into the abyss, until finally, he saw what looked like the sea floor. It was very dark, but sure enough, it was a sandy, rocky bottom. As he passed along the sea floor, he saw it! He saw the boat, the wreck of the Celebration.

It felt like a mirage as he swam towards it. But as he got closer, he saw that it was real. It was broken right in half in, two pieces, on the sea floor. For a moment, he stopped in his tracks. Were his parents inside the sailboat? He knew he wasn't ready for that. Were the people he met on the spaceship his parents? He really didn't know for sure. One thing he did know was that he was going to find out who his parents really were. It meant everything to him. It was his life's quest - to find out who they were and what had really happened. He entered the boat through the back hatch and ironically, because of the ocean's frigid temperatures, it was kept in a pristine state for over sixteen years... since that very day when they went down in the Bermuda Triangle where SeaWalker was rescued.

He was running out of air though, and he needed desperately to take a breath. As fate would have it, there was still air in the bottom of the boat, so he swam forward and gasped a few deep breaths. That was all he really needed as he continued to look throughout the cabin. And there, sitting on the floor, was a photo. The glass was a little cracked, but otherwise in flawless condition. In it, there he was a baby. It was SeaWalker sitting on the laps of his parents, Steve and Ocean. This brought a tear to his eyes. He was finally looking at his parents. It seemed the folks that he had met on the alien spacecraft resembled them remarkably. But, were they really his parents? His parents couldn't have survived this depth. But there were no bones or signs of them. His only hope was to keep searching to find the truth. What had really happened to his parents? By some miracle, were they able to survive as he had, or did they perish in the abyss? Maybe the aliens abducted them? He wasn't sure. He didn't want to give up hope. He was just so happy to finally have found the very boat that held his first memories and the last of his parents who he missed dearly. He decided it was time to head back up, so he went to the bow and grabbed a couple deep breaths of air and made his way to the surface - over 4,000 feet above!

# CHAPTER THIRTY

As soon as SeaWalker returned to the surface, he turned towards the alien spaceship. He wanted to see his parents and tell them he found the sailboat. He made a beeline for the alien ship. He arrived at the sea bottom where the space ship was resting. He just swam along until he saw two large portholes. Looking in, he saw a number of aliens sitting around discussing whatever aliens discuss. As he swam further along towards the entry, he saw another porthole. And, in this porthole, he saw what appeared to be two costumes. The costumes were eerie and upon closer inspection, they appeared to be rubber molds made in the images of his parents. In fact, they were entire body molds! Indeed, these creepy looking costumes were the parents that he had met on his last visit here. The resemblance was amazing! They were hung up on clothes hangers. At that moment, two aliens walked into the room and started talking. Fortunately, SeaWalker's hearing was so acute, he could hear what the two saying. They said that SeaWalker had been spotted in the area and that he may come by, so the two aliens quickly grabbed the costumes and swam into them. In a moment's time, they transformed and exactly resembled SeaWalker's parents. Of course, he was horrified at this! He now knew the truth. They could not have been his parents. No way!

SeaWalker was horrified, but before he could even move, something grabbed his shoulder. It was two of the alien security guards, grabbing him and pulling him towards the entry. SeaWalker resisted at first but decided it was no use and went along with the aliens. As the door opened, he was pushed inside. "Sit here for a moment. I will get the Captain."

SeaWalker heard a lot of commotion in the other room, a lot of yelling and screaming. Eventually, the door opened and the Captain came in along with what looked like his parents. "SeaWalker, we are so glad to see you! We're really glad you stopped by." His so-called parents chimed in, "SeaWalker, thank you so much for coming by. We have been thinking about you." SeaWalker replied, "I've been thinking about you too! I just saw your costume change. Yes, I saw you! I saw you actually put on costumes in order to look like my parents! That's sick! How could you?" SeaWalker dropped to his knees in pain and the costumed aliens ran over, "You didn't see what you thought you saw. We are your parents."

"Liars! Liars! You are lying. How could you do something so deceitful? Don't you know how much I care? How could you do this to me?"

The aliens knew that they had been busted. They knew the gig was up! What they didn't know was how they were going to convince SeaWalker to be with them. He alone was the link to the world above and below. He now knew these were not his parents, but who were these aliens? He bolted out of the spaceship, wiping his eyes, swimming full speed ahead to his real family... the dolphins that saved him on that fateful day.

*Humans know more about deep space than the deep ocean. It's an unknown mystery even today...*

*W*

# CHAPTER THIRTY-ONE

# PIRATE SOUL

One evening, SeaWalker joined his tribe as they started telling stories of the early days when pirates prayed on ships and plundered all their goods. They explained that pirates were real, and they were the most feared people on the high seas. These men, and sometimes women, struck terror in the hearts and souls of seafarers everywhere, including the Bermuda Triangle. The 16th and 17th centuries were the Caribbeans golden age of piracy. The elders told stories of these maritime bandits that defiled and pillaged and partied like there was no tomorrow. Rum was their drink of choice, and the Caribbean was theirs to plunder.

Many of the pirates became legends - such as Blackbeard, Captain Kidd, Black Bart and others who were bloodthirsty killers. Each seemed to take pleasure in the way they conquered their prey. Ships that carried gold where their favorite targets. If there was loot to be had, they wanted it at any cost. SeaWalker was fascinated by the stories. The folklore of pirate-life fascinated the dolphins. Their parents and grandparents told them about this unruly cast of characters, and they enjoyed hearing about the pirate's antics. The pirates considered the dolphins a good omen. The pirate-life was considered a hard one, but it paid handsomely.

But sometimes, the pirates paid with their lives. Many were killed during battles with other ships, and others drowned when their ships entered the Bermuda Triangle. Navigation was by the stars and some charts during this time. And in many cases, the fact that most were drunk on rum, using no navigational instruments, meant their lives were definitely cut short. The pirates didn't care. They were living the highlife on their own terms... literally sticking a sword in the eye of the establishment that looked down on them.

The pirates inhabiting the ghost ships that were now on the bottom of the sea in the Triangle still wreaked havoc... now on the other lost souls. They were frozen in time. The aliens were even scared of them. The dolphins felt that their energy was so tainted with rum and bad intentions that it may contaminate their species. The pirate souls roamed aimlessly in the ship graveyard still drinking rum from the barrels that sunk hundreds of years ago. SeaWalker chimed in and said, " Can we try this rum?" The elders yelled, "No, No, No! Don't even think about going near them!" Then they all laughed.

The very next day, SeaWalker's curiosity got to him, and he decided to go down and see the pirates for himself. The half day's journey lead him to the place where all the scary pirate ships were strewn about the seafloor. As he swam closer, he noticed a number of pirates huddled together around a campfire, but there was no fire. They were loud and seemed to be drunk. He tried to be stealthy, but a pirate stood up sensing that someone was near. It was Blackbeard, who had the reputation as the most notorious pirate to ever sail the high seas. At first, he pulled two pistols out of his holster, but when he saw SeaWalker, he put them away and smiled deeply. "Come here lad and join us." The pirates had always enjoyed the dolphins for entertainment, and he was now inviting one into the group. The Captain asked SeaWalker to sample the rum, but SeaWalker declined. Blackbeard insisted and they all sat down to watch SeaWalker sample his first drink of alcohol. It had a sweet taste, so he drank it straight down and asked for another. The pirates were amused at their new friend. They were fascinated by this new being that obviously had both human and dolphin characteristics. Blackbeard wanted to get him drunk so that he could interrogate him and find out what he knew. SeaWalker was also curious and looked forward to hearing more pirate stories. Blackbeard began to tell the story of how he ended up with his crew at the bottom of the Caribbean in the Bermuda Triangle. SeaWalker couldn't stop looking at this scary character with a long black beard braided with colorful beads. It was the hairiest human he had ever seen. He was a giant of a man, and his eyes were black and deep with red veins covering most of the white areas. He was dressed all in pirate gear, still carrying a multitude of guns and swords and wearing a large black pirate hat. His weapon of choice was a large dagger that he kept in his white belt. Many of his victims considered him to be the devil! It was the fear of him that really helped Blackbeard pillage more ships than any other pirate. He also plundered more gold and killed more people than anyone in pirate history. He was the Royal Navy's number one enemy! It was thought that Blackbeard was killed in a battle off the coast of North Carolina with his black flag flying high... in reality Blackbeard had escaped with a small crew. He eventually seized another pirate ship and headed towards the Bermuda Triangle. They were hit by a massive hurricane that brought the ship to rest in the graveyard below. SeaWalker began to tell his story, and the pirates decided that he was just drunk and making it up. Finally, it was time for SeaWalker to say goodbye to the crew and Blackbeard. They said, "Come visit again soon." SeaWalker assured them he would, and to save him some rum!

*If ye can't trust a Pirate, try an undead one...*

*W*

# CHAPTER THIRTY-TWO

# MEETING OF THE MINDS

**W**ith all of the weird things happening in the Triangle, the one thing that was consistent was his family. He felt like he was part of the tribe now and wanted to contribute to the wellbeing of the smartest minds in the water. Their origins began fifty million years ago and evolved into the most intelligent and dominant species in the ocean realm. Unfortunately, everything now hung in the balance for his new family as they continued to survive against all odds. Other dolphin tribes had lost entire generations due to poison from toxic levels of pollution and other human threats. The things that SeaWalker had experienced in his short life were unimaginable and new to the dolphin legacy.

Once a month, the entire tribe converged at a hidden undersea cave to have a meeting of the minds. Each member would telepathically contribute to the understanding of the state of the group and to the effort to ensure they all made it through another day.

A human could not survive one day in the unforgiving sea. They loved to enter the water, sometimes diving beneath the surface for a short period of time. But this was the world of great whales, dolphins and other aquatic life. Unfortunately for the humans, one species held their fate in their hands. One thing was for sure, everyone in SeaWalker's life knew that he somehow was important to the survival of all life. They didn't know for certain, but they felt it deep in their subconscious. SeaWalker felt it too, and when it came his time to contribute to the meeting of the minds, he shared a vision of a future that gave hope to all the animals of the ocean. He knew instinctively that it had to include the walkers. There was a reason he felt that he was at this place, at this moment in time. He believed there were no accidents, and the Universe worked in mysterious ways. Now, it was even clearer that he had to secure his role. He would spend time navigating the perils of the human race. It was a race for survival and a race that SeaWalker felt they would have to win. All the dolphins, from the young to the elders, put their heads together and created a synergy that gave the group the power and clarity they needed to go forward. After an hour, the meeting broke, and the elders headed off to their area while SeaWalker and his closest friends stayed together to dolphin storm some more ideas and strategize how they could inspire each other to continue their quest to reverse the actions of one species and work towards a global solution! Everything that occurred had led them to this moment.

The fact of the matter was that the dolphins knew. There was only one ocean; there was only one planet, and it was a water planet. If there was hope to preserve the water planet, it rested with the young walkers that SeaWalker had taken the time to get to know. SeaWalker felt deeply that a sea change could only be accomplished through these young ones. Yet, was there enough time? The acidic sea was killing entire schools of fish, and some shark species were on the brink of extinction. Extinction was something that the entire tribe feared... having heard and seen many species disappear from the planet forever.

There was a time, not long ago, when all species were hunted to near extinction. But, something happened, and the walkers somehow were changing their ways. We needed this to occur on a global scale. We needed the humans to ensure their own survival by protecting the ocean. SeaWalker decided he would plant the seeds in the hearts and minds of every human he encountered. He would plant the seeds of CONSERVATION! Without a healthy planet, nothing would survive. If only the humans could follow the traditions of the dolphins and only take what they needed and nothing more. SeaWalker had heard about early walker tribes that followed many of the same traditions. Unfortunately, they were nearly wiped out by other walkers. He saw many parallels as he continued to voyage on land, trying to understand the history and culture of these humans.

It seemed very simple - never take more than you need and try to leave the world a better place. Also, help out where you can. But, most importantly, do no harm! Even after all he had been through, SeaWalker was still optimistic. It was in his nature to see the good in all things, including humans. He decided he would remain positive and share his knowledge of the ocean world with the humans so that they may understand how to better appreciate its importance to their own existence. The fact of the matter was that walkers needed to correct some of the problems they created and reverse some of the negative impacts that were polluting, not only the oceans, but all waterways on the fragile planet. Another issue was the undersea aliens and the horror they created. Were they friend or foe? It was too early to tell, but some of the things that SeaWalker witnessed gave him pause. It was amazing to him that the humans still didn't believe in aliens or UFOs. As for SeaWalker, he believed! He had seen firsthand how the aliens had abducted humans for their own survival. Were the humans ready for SeaWalker? He wasn't sure, but he knew one day there had to be an awakening. And that day was coming soon!!

*The sea will survive without man...*

W

265

# CHAPTER THIRTY-THREE

# LAND OR SEA

It was now time for SeaWalker to and reflect on the future. He meditated for hours and hours. Would he continue to live in the sea where danger from humans and aliens was clear and present? Or should he say farewell and join his true love Marina and return to the land like his ancestors did millions of years before?

"No!" he decided. "I will live in both worlds and try to make a difference for those in the sea and on the land." Destiny was calling SeaWalker, and he felt it deeply. He would continue to share his wisdom with all life on the water planet. He had all the abilities of the great marine mammals. He also had the heart and feelings of his parents. Both would serve him well now and into the future.

Maybe not today, but one day humans would respect the sea and come to realize water is sacred and connects all life - from the smallest plankton to the largest animals that inhabited the earth, the blue whales. Would we now begin to finally protect the heart of the blue planet, our ocean? Water was the one element that connected all the people and animals on land and in the sea. Without water, nothing would survive. The planet was being pushed towards a future that was void of life. The air was toxic; the forests were being destroyed faster than they could be replenished, and the ocean was dying.

There were actually floating islands of plastic... PLASTIC! There was war and conflicts among people from different nations who must share the same limited resources on an ever-smaller planet. A well-known marine biologist and hero for the planet, Dr. Sylvia Earle, had said, "What we humans do in the next ten years will determine the next 10,000." There had never been a clearer call to action. If the planet and its inhabitants were to survive, everyone needed to do their part. It was a race to save all of the species living on the water planet! SeaWalker had heard the call. One thing was for sure, the world was changing. A new day had come. All must embrace the natural world or go the way of the dinosaurs. SeaWalker lived so that others could survive, giving hope to all species.

SeaWalker floated on the surface, in a trance, imagining his future. Suddenly, out of the night sky, a beam of blinding light came from high above. It focused directly over SeaWalker. The light beam paralyzed his body. He was frozen. Next, the light drew him slowly up towards the alien spaceship. The light was so bright it nearly blinded him. It took him from the sea and the earth and pulled him towards the alien mother ship located

# LAND OR SEA

a half-mile above the direct center of the Bermuda Triangle - 25.000° N, 71.000° W.

As SeaWalker was pulled weightlessly towards the light emanating from the bottom of the immense spaceship, it drew SeaWalker into the vessel. He continued to be levitated until his body was turned horizontal and placed on a cold, stainless steel operating table. A half-dozen strange looking alien beings hovered over him. They were all wearing surgical masks to cover up their two holes where a nose might be and a larger round hole in the center of the chin. Their large, black bug-like eyes seemed to look right through their new visitor. Suddenly, his entire life flashed before him! He felt his mind being manipulated as the aliens tried to reassure him that he was in no harm. They placed a needle into a vein in his arm, and suddenly, everything went blank...

*TO BE CONTINUED...*

# SeaWalker - Ocean Wisdom

Dolphins are ocean angels and our guide to another world...

The ocean without borders is truly a whale nation...

Water is life...

The sea is the genesis of all life...

Great Leviathan, ruler of the sea...

Our planet is blue...

The ocean covers 7/10 of the surface of our water planet...

Viewed from space, we see an ocean planet...

The oceans are the domain of great whales...

Whales have evolved over a 50 million years, with the largest brains on the earth...

The true territory of the planet is not the domain of humans but great whales...

Man continues to have domain over the great whales even though they have smaller brains...

Whales are weightless in their world and fly through the ocean more graceful than birds...

Humans would not last more than a few minutes in the unforgiving sea where whales have thrived for 50 million years...

Larger brains and bodies that have evolved without destroying their environment...

Great whales float in the buoyant sea, unrestricted by gravity -angels of the ocean realm...

Swim naked in the buoyant sea, weightless and unencumbered by the restrictions of land...

The dolphins are my family and the ocean is my playground...

With ease, I can breach the surface, soring 30 feet in the air and returning to the life-giving sea...

In the sea, we are free...except for many...

The sea gives eternal joy and inspires the imagination...

The ocean is a symphony of music created by whales that have continued to evolve their songs to communicate to one another, but more importantly to inspire...

Each year, the humpback whale adds new melodies to their song that began 50 million years ago...

Spirits of the deep awaken to a new resident born of the land and the sea...

Even today, the ocean has not revealed all her secrets...

Mermaids began as land creatures who entered the sea and decided to never leave...

The mermaids, like SeaWalker today, are considered a myth until now...

As on land and in the sea, different dialects exist between all the species but are understood by one, SeaWalker...

Whales are considered alien beings until you meet the real aliens from space...

Whale and dolphin families are ancient tribes without Borders, and the ocean is their nation...

SeaWalker is a force of nature...

SeaWalker has the accumulated knowledge of the past and the ability to see the future...

SeaWalker lives in a sea of sound...

Echolocation allows SeaWalker to see accurate pictures of predators in the pitch black, deep oceans allowing him to prosper and survive...

How ironic that the largest creature, the blue whale, eats some of the smallest the plankton to amass a size of over 100 feet and 200 tons...

The largest creature ever to have lived could only survive in the buoyancy of the sea, but is now threatened by one species man...

The intelligence of dolphins and whales cannot be measured by man...

Dolphins and whales are guided by an internal compass navigating by the stars and ocean currents...

SeaWalker's compass is in his brain...

SeaWalker's ability to navigate the mass of ocean realm and the land is exclusive to him...

SeaWalker's sonar and inner compass give him superiority over his domain...

Herculean strength and speed with superior intelligence is SeaWalker...

The fastest animal on land is the cheetah in the sea the Sailfish, until now were SeaWalker holds that distinction...

The pulse and rhythm of the sea is in every fiber of this new species, long live SeaWalker...

SeaWalker has the ability to dive at the depths even great whales find impossible...

SeaWalker can stay submerged where even great Whales must surface to inhale the life-giving air above...

Whales and dolphins are not a product to be exploited by man but true ancient tribes inhabiting the oceans long before man...

In ancient Greece, dolphins were considered Gods...

The sovereignty and dignity of whales must be respected by man...

The health of the oceans is critical to our life on land; they are intricately connected...

People are ignorant of the impact they're having on the health of the planet...

In Greek times, the killing of a dolphin was the same as killing a man and punishable the same as murder...

Whales celebrate the pure joy of living in the present...

Cetaceans have involved with the abilities that humans will never acquire...

Dolphin societies include up to ten generations. living at the same time...

We now know that there is another intelligence that lives not on land but in the sea...

Minds in the waters that have involved over 50 million years...

# ABOUT THE AUTHOR

SeaWalker is acclaimed artist, writer, filmmaker and conservationist Wyland's first book of fiction. He is planning a trilogy of books and films featuring this amazing new creature, who is both of the land and the sea.

Aliens who have secretly been plotting the earth's takeover have been here from the beginning of time and now have begun an assault on the planet. The story takes place in the mysterious Bermuda Triangle where aliens have their home base and are taking human souls. The strange disappearances are revealed when SeaWalker discovers an alien-populated factory near a ship graveyard that is processing the undead for unimaginable experiments. So here we go into the unknown, a future that looks grim. What will happen, let's Sea...

# ABOUT THE ILLUSTRATIONS

The original paintings for the cover "Storm" and "Sea Walker" for the back cover were conceived by the artist along with a series of original silver point illustrations for each chapter for a new trilogy of sci-fi books and films.

Wyland Worldwide, LLC
509 S. Coast Hwy • Laguna Beach, CA
www.wyland.com